P9-AQV-575

THE RETREAT

BOOKS BY

AHARON APPELFELD

Badenheim 1939

The Age of Wonders

Tzili: The Story of a Life

The Retreat

To the Land of the Cattails

The Immortal Bartfuss

For Every Sin

The Healer

Katerina

Unto the Soul

*Beyond Despair: Three Lectures and a
Conversation with Philip Roth*

The Iron Tracks

THE RETREAT

AHARON APPELFELD

Translated from the Hebrew by Dalya Bilu

Schocken Books   New York

FEB - 2 1998

Copyright © 1984 by Aharon Appelfeld

All rights reserved under International and Pan-American
Copyright Conventions. Published in the United States by
Schocken Books Inc., New York, and simultaneously in
Canada by Random House of Canada Limited, Toronto.
Distributed by Pantheon Books, a division of Random House,
Inc., New York. Originally published in the United States in
hardcover by E. P. Dutton, Inc., New York, in 1984.

SCHOCKEN and colophon are trademarks of Schocken Books Inc.

Library of Congress Cataloging-in-Publication Data

Appelfeld Aron.
The retreat / Aharon Appelfeld;
translated from the Hebrew by Dalya Bilu.
p. cm.
Previously published: 1st ed. New York : Dutton, c1984.
ISBN 0-8052-1096-2
I. Bilu, Dalya. II. Title.
PJ5054.A765R4 1998 892.4'36—dc21 97-28634 CIP

Random House Web Address: http://www.randomhouse.com

Printed in the United States of America

First Schocken Paperback Edition 1998

9 8 7 6 5 4 3 2 1

THE RETREAT

ONE

They drove south in an old coach on a dirt road. One after the other the landscapes slipped past, the summer in all its glory, suffocating with the weight of its scents and sap. Now they turned and began to climb the mountain. The coachman drove the horses slowly, without goading them on. For many hours the mother and daughter had not exchanged a single word, leaning back on the shabby seat, each sunk in her own thoughts.

Suddenly the mother said, "Where are we going? I don't understand." She said these words without turning her head. The daughter did not respond. Her strained face creased in something resembling a smile.

1

"I asked you a question," said the mother.

"I don't understand, Mother."

At the sound of these words the mother jerked her head sharply round, threw her daughter a look, and leaned her head back against the seat without another word. The daughter covered her forehead with her right hand.

For two months the quarrel between them had raged. Now all that was left was an echo, not lacking in sharpness, however. The storm refused to subside.

The plateau unrolled before them, flat, broad and cultivated. The trees were bright green. The mother was familiar with these passing landscapes from her travels. She had never examined them at close quarters, always too busy and burdened. Now the charming scenes seemed to approach and beckon, pressing up against her eyes, but she was tense and irritated, waiting impatiently for the end of this journey, which for some reason was dragging on and on. The coachman and his horses had joined forces against her.

"I don't understand why it was necessary for you to trouble yourself. There are places to which a person should travel alone," said the mother in a low voice, with great restraint.

"I won't let you go alone."

"Please don't exaggerate," said the mother, tightening her lips.

The truth was that it had been her own decision

to come here. At first her daughter had pretended to oppose the idea but in the end she had consented, she didn't care any more. Now all they wanted was to get away from each other. But the coachman, as if to spite them, refused to hurry. He drove the horses slowly, in a kind of calm indifference, as if he had all the time in the world.

"Is it still far to go?" the mother asked him impatiently.

"A fair way."

"In that case, will you make your horses go faster, please."

"The horses are not used to dirt roads," said the coachman in a heavy, rustic voice. "They've grown accustomed to city ways, for our sins." He pronounced the last word in the old-fashioned, religious way.

"And if I give you something extra, will you urge them on?"

"What are you talking about?" the daughter interrupted.

"It's none of your business," said the mother in the way she used to speak to her when she was a child.

"I am not in the habit of goading my horses," said the coachman. "This is a bad road. What's the matter, aren't the seats comfortable?"

"No, to tell the truth," said the mother in a voice left over from bygone days, a capricious voice.

"I won't change my ways for you, my lady.

3

Money can't buy everything, you know. Horses deserve our pity too."

"Horses are more important to you, I see, than people."

"The creator created them too, did he not?"

The mother knew this tone only too well, with its infuriating affectation of piety.

The daughter said, "What's the point of arguing."

"I'm still allowed to talk, aren't I? I won't give up the right to talk."

"Do as you please," said the daughter, and held her tongue.

The horses trudged heavily on. The old coachman muttered to himself, "The devil only knows why I let them tempt me. This road wasn't made for coaches, it's fit only for cattle." The mother knew there was nothing serious in this complaint. All he wanted was to put the price up. She laughed. The daughter was surprised by her laughter and said, "What's so funny?"

"Can't you hear?"

The coachman turned his head and said, "I wouldn't make this climb again for all the money in the world." And in truth the road was tortuous, steep and full of stones, but the scenery on both sides was magnificent in its simplicity.

In the winter of 1937 the mother had still played a few small parts in the theater. And that was the end. No one had given a farewell party for her, and it soon transpired that her pension too was in ques-

4

tion. For a few months she ran from place to place, called on old friends, knocked on doors. In the end, penniless and at the end of her tether, she arrived on her daughter's doorstep. Her daughter did her best but her husband, George, did not make her welcome. He did not think much of actors.

For two weeks she stayed in her daughter's house, upsetting everyone and even quarreling with her grandsons. Her daughter stood between them, buffeted by the storms. One night the mother announced: "I can't stay here," and she left.

Her daughter caught up with her at the station. For a few days they ran around the town together. Once more she called on old friends, visited labor exchanges. She was determined: I must work, never mind at what. But no one was prepared to employ an aging actress, not even as a shop assistant. They were on the point of going back. The daughter promised to have it out with her husband. Everything would be all right. On their way to the station they encountered the old headmaster of the high school. He was regarded as a liberal, broad-minded man. Seeing the two women in their distress he said, "I have an idea. Not far from here is a mountain retreat, a spiritual center on a sublime peak. I myself once took part in one of their debates. If I'm not mistaken, there is a very satisfactory hotel there too."

That was the place, they all agreed.

On their way home she regretted her haste. She

suspected that the place was some kind of Jewish home. Questions again, and endless talk—she had always loathed them. But when they got back, late that night, she quickly realized that anything was better than this hell, even a Jewish retreat.

"When will we arrive?" the mother roused herself from her thoughts and asked the coachman.

"Early this evening, God willing."

"Why bother God all the time," said the mother impatiently, sick of all this affected piety.

"What can I do? We still hold by the old ways and still believe in Him. And you, I take it, are an unrepentant atheist."

"Yes," said the mother, deliberately provocative.

"I," said the peasant in a peasant voice, "would never dare provoke Him on such a steep, bumpy road."

"I'm too old to change now," said the mother impatiently.

"I understand," said the coachman.

In her heart she admired this primitive rawness. Once upon a time, when she was still a young woman, she had entered into conversation with them on the course of her travels, and sometimes she had teased them too. Over the years she had come to know their language, their stupidity and also their wisdom.

The short exchange with the old coachman gave her back a fleeting taste of different, younger days, and she asked, "Have you never been up there before?"

6

"Never. Who lives there?"

"Jews."

"And you are going to them?"

"Yes."

"I can't believe my eyes."

"What can I do about it?"

"But you don't look like a Jewess, my lady."

"Nevertheless, the truth can no longer be concealed."

The daughter sat huddled in her corner without saying a word, full of resentment at the length of the journey, her mother's endless chatter, and all the trouble she had caused her in the past few months. The thought that many more scandals were still in store preyed on her mind. She longed for her home and her children.

"Mother," she said, without any special emotion.

"What?" The mother pricked up her ears.

"Don't forget to write to me."

"You know I don't like writing letters. Writing letters drives me out of my mind."

"Only a word or two."

"Nothing bad is going to happen to me. When all's said and done, the Jews aren't going to do me any harm." She pronounced the word "Jews" the way gentiles pronounced it.

"As you wish," said the daughter. "You must do as you see fit." In her arguments with her mother she always came off second best.

The afternoon hour hung silently over the plateau. The ascent was gradual but they could sense quite clearly that the air was already different, sharp and intoxicating. The expression on the daughter's tense face grew more and more frozen. The events of recent months, which had begun by embarrassing her, had ended by filling her with rage. As for the mother, the expression on her face kept on changing until it settled into one of pride. Her daughter knew this expression well. It always gave her a disagreeable feeling—her own inferiority.

Her mother was, indeed, better educated than she was. She had not read much in recent years, but the knowledge she had accumulated in high school and later on at the acting academy served her as a hidden treasure trove: modern literature and the classics, theater and music. The daughter too had graduated from high school, but it was only a commercial college, which made no attempt at providing a humanist education but was content to turn out respectable housewives. And that's what she was, a housewife: she had reared three sons, she cooked hearty meals for her husband and did the family washing at night. The mother exploited her advantage to the utmost, and occasionally ridiculed her daughter's ignorance. The coachman now knew that he would be paid extra for the journey, and he was content. He did not urge the horses on, but neither did he grumble.

"And what have they got up there?" he asked in the tone of a domestic servant who permitted himself a personal question from time to time.

"A spiritual center," said the mother, knowing that the coachman would not understand the meaning of the words.

"I don't understand," said the coachman.

"Have you never heard of Martin Buber?" She now addressed him as she would a servant of her own age.

"No, my lady, never."

"I beg you, engrave the name upon your heart. You'll thank me for whispering it in your ear one day."

"Thank you, my lady. Is the gentleman a priest, or a saint?"

"A philosopher."

"A philosopher. I understand."

The mother, to tell the truth, had never taken much interest in these famous names. From her youth she had felt an aversion for all things Jewish. Jewish actors and writers counted for nothing in her eyes. She loved the classics, the living vernacular, speech without sophistry. Now all this too was remote from her, all she wanted was to amuse the coachman and forget herself for a moment. And the coachman was happy to respond to her invitation.

"I've known many a Jew in my time. You might say I know them well. And it seems to me that I can tell them from a distance. But you, my lady, look so much like one of us that if I had to swear on it, I would swear."

"Appearances are deceptive, not so?" said the mother softly.

9

"But to such an extent. I would never have guessed."

"The devil isn't as black as he's painted."

"I agree with you, my lady, with all my heart," said the coachman ingratiatingly.

"What is it that makes them so different?" she inquired in an interested tone.

"Nothing at all," he said slyly.

"You're exaggerating, I think."

"All men are equal in His eyes, not so?"

"And yet, the Jew is still a Jew."

"The Jew is a merchant. And what of it if he is. But you, my lady, do not possess a single Jewish feature."

"Thank you."

"I mean it in all seriousness. You're a fine-looking woman."

"That's ridiculous," said the mother, and burst out laughing.

The conversation proceeded pleasantly enough. The coachman, a sturdy fellow, told her that he had left home as a lad because of a quarrel over a trifle and gone to town. At first he had worked as a porter and a hired coachman. Now he was independent. The mother knew that this tale was not as innocent as it sounded. The trifling quarrel, in all proba-bility, meant that he had stolen his father's money and perhaps wasted it on drink as well. Over the years, during the course of her many travels, she had learned to listen to them and to like their crude naïveté, the way they mixed up fact with fantasy.

The coachman stopped the horses and said, "Time for a little rest." The daughter woke from her trance and said, "What are you thinking of? It's already three o'clock."

"What of it."

"I have to get home on time."

"We'll get there. Don't you worry about the time."

"I am worried about it."

"When a man sets out on a journey he should leave his watch at home. He knows the hour of his departure, but never the hour of his return. Time is in the hands of the creator."

"I don't know what you're talking about."

"My dear lady," he said, turning his head around to enlist the support of the mother, "explain the meaning of time to her. We of the older generation know what it means, not so?"

At this the daughter jerked her head sharply and said in a voice full of angry indignation, "You promised us that we'd be there by three. And just look where we are now. I have a home and children waiting for me."

"Take it easy, my lady," said the coachman in an offensive drawl. "It's a wise man who knows the truth of the saying 'Man proposes but God disposes.' Isn't that so?"

The mother did not rush to her daughter's aid. She was busy watching the coachman's hands. He took the fodder bags out of the box and tied them to the horses' heads, muttering to himself, "They're hungry. They're hungry." She was enchanted by the movements of his hands, so quiet they were hardly perceptible.

"And you, have you nothing to say to him?" The daughter turned on her mother.

"What is there to say? Can't you see, he's feeding his horses."

"And I left the house alone, the children."

Who asked you to, she wanted to say, but on seeing her daughter's strained face she controlled herself and said, "It won't be long now. It won't be long."

The daughter ground her teeth.

The mother thrust her neck out of her coat collar and scrutinized her daughter. Her only daughter, her love and her hope. All that was good and maternal in her she had yearned to give her. True, the theater and the provincial tours had taken her away from home, but all her leisure hours, and there were many of them, had been devoted to her daughter. She had been a quiet, obedient child who read a lot and at the age of eight even showed signs of a certain musical gift. This discovery filled the mother's heart with a secret joy. She herself would take her to her lessons and watch her play. At the age of twelve, for no apparent reason, she abandoned the piano and refused to continue her lessons. For a few weeks the mother had coaxed her but when she persisted in her refusal, the mother left her alone. She enrolled in the commercial college and her grades were satisfactory. When she turned fifteen her face changed, her nose lengthened, her mouth tightened: a strange seriousness. In the mother's heart there was no doubt: the features forming the young face were her father's. This distressed her, of course.

The daughter grew up and year by year her face changed. Her nature was placid and lacking in any inner fire. She went on reading and going to concerts like any other middle-class girl, but she was not Lotte's daughter—a girl with no passions or ambitions. At the age of twenty she married a man ten years older than herself, an Austrian by birth with a small country estate.

In the meantime the coachman finished feeding the horses. The horses did not look very lively. They seemed sleepy. He himself sat down on the ground and prepared a modest meal: breed, white cheese and a raw cucumber. The fresh bread smelled of the oven in which it had been baked.

"Aren't you eating?" He turned to the mother.

"I'm not hungry."

"You seem sad."

"A little tired."

"May I offer you a little cheese? Excellent cheese, if I say so myself."

"Thank you."

"We still eat the old, simple food," the coachman apologized, not without a hint at the corruption of city life. Now he spoke to her like an old acquaintance. He knew the country inns and innkeepers.

And the customers too, actors and directors. He knew as well as the mother did that there was no innocence in all these. Corruption had spread everywhere.

"We can continue now," said the coachman, after saying a short blessing.

It was four o'clock. The tall trees cast their shade over the road, which stretched ahead like a cool tunnel. The daughter wrapped herself in a shawl with a movement which showed suppressed rage.

"You're uneasy, I see," said the mother. "I'm sorry I let you come."

The daughter, her anger bursting out, said, "I haven't got the faintest desire to get into an argument with you. You know very well that I left the children without anyone to look after them."

"Exactly as I said, you shouldn't have come. I would have managed without you."

"You would have wasted all the money." The daughter flung the words from her mouth.

"I?" said the mother, who did not care to examine the meaning of these words too closely.

"Yes, you." The daughter cast compunction to the winds.

Now it seemed that the mother was about to pull the bundle of banknotes from her purse and tear them to shreds or throw them in her daughter's face. But for some reason she did not do so.

"Thank you," she said.

"You know perfectly well how I fought with

14

George. And I must say that he behaved with the patience of a saint. There's a limit to whims and caprices. How much money can one person waste?"

George, ever since she had come to know him intimately, had revolted her. A petit bourgeois Austrian who worshiped money, like his fathers before him. A born miser to whom every form of assistance to others, especially financial assistance, seemed a blatant breach of the social contract, the heart and soul of which was: let every man endure his fate in silence, without turning the world upside down.

"George, you say," said the mother.

"You were always extravagant."

This word, which she hated with all her heart, was too much for her to bear. Her face twisted and her voice, intending sharpness, thickened instead as she said, "Extravagance is in my nature. And I'm proud of it."

"Oh yes, I know."

"Extravagance is a human quality, too human perhaps. Only rodents hoard. What remains to us in this life if we can't waste a little money, since in any case we haven't got too much to waste?"

"And the future." Her daughter tightened her lips obstinately.

"The future? Where did you get that disgusting word from? What does it mean? Where is this future of yours?"

The bitter smile relaxed a little on her daughter's

lips. Now it seemed that she was about to smile broadly, a real smile. But it was only an illusion: her back stiffened.

The mother continued: "The future. We, thank God, are free of that hypocrisy. As long as we've got a penny in our pocket we'll spend it. Spend it freely. Don't dare pronounce that detestable word in my presence again."

The daughter said defiantly, "Because of your extravagance you've always been poor. You've got nothing, no property, not even a pension."

"What of it? Men come into the world without security, without insurance, without pensions, and they die without them too. Can't you get that into your head? And as for your money—don't worry. You'll get it all back."

"I'm not worried."

"And now I'm going to the Jews. You know yourself how unwillingly. But one thing I have to admit, they have more generosity."

"And George isn't generous."

"No, definitely not."

During her short stay in her daughter's house she had observed him closely. Suspicious, with no ideas of his own and no imagination. He would sit for hours in front of the mirror combing his hair. A number of words, she noticed, were always on his lips: everything is in order, and other words which smacked of warehouses and stables.

The sun was sinking. On the green slopes forest

16

clearings gleamed here and there. The sky was cloudless. The daughter's anger seemed to leave her. She looked at the scenery.

"Not far now," said the coachman, who had been listening attentively to the exchange between the two women. I'm in no hurry, the mother wanted to say, but knowing that this remark would enrage her daughter beyond bearing, she said instead, "Good." She now wanted to resume her conversation with the coachman. And he apparently sensed her wish and responded at once, as follows: "When I was a lad I used to take a lot of Jewish merchants to the railway station. They always tipped me. They're more generous than we are, I must admit."

"But you don't like them."

"I don't know why."

She was fond of such men, in spite of everything. In her travels in the provinces she had shown them her favors more than once. She had seen them in her imagination as the incarnation of nature, of simplicity. She was soon disillusioned, of course. They were not as simple as she imagined.

They were approaching the peak. The daughter now wished to mend matters a little and she said, "I'll come and visit you." The mother noticed that she did not say, We'll come and visit you. It was better that way, without George.

"Don't bother," she said.

Now, for some reason, she took pity on her daughter, who was encumbered with three hulking sons and a husband who demanded his meals on time. The sons, like their father, were dull and healthy and had nothing in their heads but swimming, football and breeding horses. At school they did not shine. Like their father they too would breed horses, and in the evenings they would sit in the inn and drink beer. The thought that her grandsons would be common, ordinary Austrians, eating and drinking their fill, brought a wry smile to her lips. During the time she had spent in their house she had come to understand something she had not previously understood: how different she was.

"Don't bother. I really mean it. When all's said and done, you've got a home and children of your own to look after."

"And don't I deserve a little holiday," her daughter surprised her by saying.

"On the contrary." Something quickened in the mother. "I've always been in favor of holidays," and as she said this her heart seemed to open inside her. "You need a rest too."

The daughter's expression softened and she said, "The house is like a millstone round my neck. Those boys are sucking my blood."

"Just what I said. You need a holiday. A man is not a beast of burden, after all." And in a whisper she added, "Come and stay up here with me." The whispered words stirred all her latent maternal feelings. Tears gathered in her eyes.

"I'll come," said the daughter.

18

Now the coach was climbing to the top of the mountain. The road was straight but steep.

"What godforsaken places the Jews choose for themselves," the coachman permitted himself to say frankly. "What do they do here?"

"They think," said Lotte teasingly.

"What have they got to think about so much?"

"All kinds of things," said Lotte lightly.

"If it wasn't for you, my lady, I'd turn the horses round. Who's going to pay me to mend the wheels?"

"Don't worry. Nobody lives for ever," she said, adopting his manner of speaking.

All that remained of the daughter's frozen expression was one line creasing her forehead. She was close to tears. Her mother sensed this and said, "Take a holiday at the first opportunity. Come here and we'll enjoy ourselves together. The scenery here is magnificent."

"What will you do here?" The daughter sought to share her fears with her mother.

"Don't worry, I've never been bored in my life. I'm dying to read a good book. All these years I've been running. Now I'll sit and read, I'll sit and contemplate my navel. And let the rest of the world go to hell."

Her daughter knew this tone well, a mixture of affectation, pride and boasting. But now her voice sounded softer. As if her loneliness had caught up with her at last.

The journey was over. The border was drawn. These above and those below. Years of sorrow gathered into a ball in the daughter's heart. All her mother's caprices were pardoned in an instant. She wanted to help her but she didn't know how. She fell on her purse and hastily removed a bundle of banknotes. "Take this, Mother."

"No, I won't take it," said her mother. "You know me."

"I won't leave you here without money."

"I have enough. There's no need for anything more up here."

"And if you want to come down, if you want to visit me."

"I'll get a ride. I'm used to hitching rides."

"Do me a favor," begged the daughter.

"You know me too well," said the mother. "I'm incurably extravagant. If I take it I'll only waste it."

"I'll keep it for you." The daughter found a way out.

"Good, you do that," the mother agreed.

The coachman stopped the coach and called, "We've arrived at last." The mother's face expressed exaggerated surprise, as if he had said something quite out of place. "Where are we?" she said in alarm, as if she were repeating a line from a play.

"This is it," said the coachman, and climbed down from his perch. He went to the box and took out a medium-sized green suitcase. The daughter too made haste to get out. The day faded into its last, blue colors. Dense shadows covered the ground, hiding the building from the eyes of the new arrivals. But a second look soon made it out. A two-storied house, not especially grand, covered in creepers. "This is it." The mother repeated the coachman's words.

"There's no one here," said the daughter.

"They're inside, someone will see me in a minute," the mother said, recovering her voice.

"I'll go in with you," offered the daughter.

"There's no need. I'm used to it."

The coachman was now waiting for his tip. The mother recognized this expectant stance at once. She immediately took a banknote out of her purse and held it out to him.

"I'll pay," said the daughter quickly.

"Of course you'll pay. That was something extra from me. The man did his best, not so?"

The coachman took off his cap and bowed.

"Come and visit me," the mother said lightly, as if they were parting after a cup of coffee in a café. The daughter embraced her mother with both arms and buried her head for a moment in her bosom.

"Time to leave," cried the coachman, and leaped nimbly onto his perch. "It was a pleasure to meet you, my lady," he said with a nod of his head. The mother narrowed her eyes and raised her hand. "Adieu, adieu," she repeated in a whisper.

"What shall I send you," cried the daughter in a choked voice.

"Nothing at all. Nothing at all."

"A coat. It must be cold up here in winter."

And the coach dashed off. For a while she stood listening to the rumble of the wheels. In the gathering darkness she no longer saw anything but her daughter's hands, hardworking hands swollen with water.

TWO

"So we've arrived," she said, as she was in the habit of saying when the company arrived at their hotel. There was no answering voice from within. The darkness drifted close to the ground, like skeins of black wool. She pushed the door open with her shoulder, a movement she had perfected over the years. But the door did not swing back automatically behind her, apparently lacking the spring usually attached to hotel entrance doors.

"Lotte Schloss," she announced in a formal tone.

"Who?" A man raised his eyes.

"Lotte Schloss." She raised her voice as if she were addressing a deaf person. Most doormen were deaf, the thought crossed her mind.

"There's no need to speak so loudly," he said in a gentle voice.

23

"I beg your pardon," said Lotte, surprised.

The man was sitting at the table with his hands folded in front of him. The table had no writing materials on it.

"Is this the Institute for Advanced Studies?" asked Lotte, pronouncing each word distinctly.

"It is."

"I've come to join."

The man's withdrawn expression changed. He opened his eyes and said, "Welcome."

She wanted to ask: What happens here, how, but when she saw the man's pale, somewhat strained face she said simply, "Where do I register?"

"With me," said the man. He took an exercise book out of the drawer and wrote: Lotte Schloss.

"What else?" she asked.

"Nothing at all."

"It couldn't be simpler," she said.

"And now we must provide you with two blankets, two sheets and a pillow."

"And a key, don't I get a key?" said Lotte in the old, coquettish way.

"No need, madam," said the man, his long, pale face brightening, as if at the sight of an attractive woman. "It's quite safe here."

"Where is everyone?" she asked with an absent-minded air.

"In the hall."

"How interesting," said Lotte.

Now she waited for him to offer her some tidbit of

24

gossip, for nothing, she knew, escaped the eyes of these doormen. And, indeed, he rose to his feet and with an air of old-fashioned politeness offered her his chair, but then for some reason he changed his mind and said, "With your permission, I'll bring you a chair."

"Mayn't I see my room?" she said in her own voice.

"Certainly, but first we must fetch you blankets, sheets and a pillow." Now she remarked a kind of spirituality carved the lines of his long face. She knew and liked such faces from her travels. Sometimes she would fall deep into conversation with such men. But for the most part she was preoccupied with the appetites of the moment, or too tired. In the meantime he went out and came back with two blankets, two sheets and a pillow, which he placed upon the table. "The bedding may not be very splendid, but it is clean, if I may say so."

Lotte noticed that the man had a soft spot for adjectives.

"Your name rings a bell, madam, but I can't remember where I heard it."

"Up to a few months ago I was an actress in the provincial theater. Not a well-known name, exactly. Chambermaids for the most part, and in recent years moralizing old servant maids."

The man bowed his head.

Lotte continued: "Did I deserve more? I don't know. Lately I've begun to believe in fate. At our

25

age we tend to become superstitious, not so? And whom have I the honor of addressing?"

"Herbert Zuntz," said the man modestly.

"Pardon me," said Lotte, sensing that she had gone too far.

"What for?"

"For imposing so many words on a new acquaintance."

"We're used to it."

"I, at any rate," said Lotte with a return of her old pride, "dislike confessions. If that is the custom here, I have come to the wrong place."

"Don't be afraid, madam. You will be able to exploit your solitude to the full here, if you so wish. The peak is glorious, the scenery sublime."

"Wonderful," she said. "And are there any services here?"

"Yes, but on a modest scale."

"No need to overdo things," she said. The new dress, a green woollen dress which her daughter had bought her as a hasty peace offering, pinched her waist, and she made a movement with her shoulder and said, "Are you a Jew too, sir?"

"I can't say unhappily and I can't say happily, so shall we say—what can we say?"

Lotte laughed, and in order to make her position quite clear she said, "I'm an actress, an actress and nothing more."

Herbert took the bedding in one hand and picked up the suitcase in the other. In doing so he revealed himself to be a man of imposing stature, and a mature distinction it was possible to fall in love with at first sight.

The place reminded her of a seedy hotel, yellowing mirrors in the bathrooms, broken toilet bowls and dripping taps, where the chambermaids spoke in impertinent voices and the doormen reached out to them with big, strong hands. In such rundown places she had spent the best years of her life. Undeniably, they had their charms. But in recent years these charms had faded. The torn mattresses, the food. Life on the road had wrought havoc with her body. People had stopped calling her by her name and started calling her the actress, and the meaning of this epithet in such places was only too clear.

They crossed a passage, an entrance lobby, went downstairs, and were immediately greeted by the following sight: people sitting round low tables, illuminated by oil lamps, playing cards. The silence was so tense you could cut it with a knife.

"Wonderful," said Herbert, as if he were seeing this scene for the first time. "You play poker?"

"No," said Lotte, surprised by the silent scene.

"Neither do I. Wonderful, the way they forget themselves. You see that old man, only a few weeks ago he was lying in bed without a hope in the world. He was revived, believe it or not, by poker. See how he pulls out the cards and throws them on the table. They say he's an outstanding player. An inspiring sight, don't you think?"

27

From here they returned to the entrance lobby, the passage, and turned right to the stairs. Herbert opened the door and lit a match. It was a long, narrow room with a window at one end and a bed against the wall. There was a bureau and a desk.

"It's not too terrible," said Lotte carelessly.

"I'll light the oil lamp and you'll see better."

A world without electricity. The thought crossed Lotte's mind that it was like a country village. She thought of the rural inns with their roofs thatched with straw, their courtyards noisy with chickens, dogs barking, the stove in the passage blazing hot and smelling of freshly baked bread.

Herbert said, "The room is not very grand, as you will discover by daylight, but it's yours."

"Thank you," said Lotte, sensing the tears gathering in her eyes. She was tired after the long day, the journey and the emotions.

Herbert placed the oil lamp on the table, said goodnight, and retired.

She longed for sleep, but pictures from recent days rose before her eyes as if to spite her; trudging up and down the streets, the employment agencies, the officials, the embarrassing questions. In the whole of the little town where she had spent her childhood, youth and maturity, nobody wanted her. Not even the streets. They all avoided her as if she had some infectious disease, and yet she was nicely dressed, in her new dress, and her hair was freshly combed. Ever since her dismissal, her disgrace seemed to have become public knowledge. I'm an actress, a professional actress, as nobody can deny. I've entertained this town to the best of my ability, in small roles, admittedly, but not insignificant nevertheless. Ignored and avoided by everyone, she poured out her wrath on her daughter. Her daughter followed her like a sleepwalker, from street to street and alley to alley. And as if in a dream she clenched her fists and gritted her teeth, knocked on all the doors and blamed her daughter for all the misfortunes that had come upon her. Her daughter did not answer back, she tried to calm her down. When she saw that her mother was beside herself with anger, she suggested: Come home and have a cup of coffee. But this proposal infuriated her the more.

Only now did the mother understand what she had done. She wanted to get up and write her a long letter, beg her pardon, promise her that from now on she would take care to behave properly. But she did not get up. She was too tired. Or rather, she was beyond tiredness. The vivid scenes of the night had weakened her.

At midnight she rose. She took a writing pad out of her bag and wrote: Dear Julia, forgive your mother. More than this she could not coax out of her pen. She sat by the desk for a long time. The quiet, narrow room calmed the commotion inside her. Suddenly, as in days gone by, she stood up and took off her clothes and stood in front of the mirror.

THREE

"They've closed the hatch." A strident female voice woke her. Lotte opened her eyes and the dream dissolved. She sensed only this: she had been very far away inside herself. The smell, without the pictures, lingered on inside her for a long time. There was a commotion in the passage. The cook, it seemed, had closed the hatch. No coffee after nine o'clock, let the latecomers learn a lesson. People stood in the passage, half awake, baffled expressions on their faces. A few stood in a corner and made fun of the situation. One woman, elegantly dressed, approached the hatch and banged on it with her fists: "Coffee. I will not be deprived of my morning coffee." She voiced her protest with a kind of grim severity, as if she were speaking of an obvious injustice. There was no response from within.

On the walls painted slogans hung next to a notice board and an ancient portrait of the Emperor.

"Have you just arrived?" One of the men approached her.

"Last night, only last night."

"A newcomer, in that case."

"Of my own free will," she said, in the manner to which she was accustomed.

"I've been here for six months already."

The scene reminded Lotte of an army canteen hastily set up in some deserted barracks hall. But here everything was more brightly lit. A healthy mind in a healthy body, it said on one of the walls. So there are gymnastics here, said Lotte to herself.

"Where from," asked the man in a whisper.

"From Wirzbaden, not far from here."

"A charming spot, no two opinions about it."

The man's closeness embarrassed her. She had not even had time to look at her face in the mirror. Unwashed and unpowdered. Her new dress creased. The thought that her dress was creased and her face unpowdered made her forget for a moment her thirst for a cup of coffee.

The man said, "I used to visit Wirzbaden as a young man. A charming spot. An excellent theater too, as I recall, for a provincial town.

"Indeed." Lotte opened her eyes wide. "I work there myself."

"Wonderful," said the man, and bowed. "As far as I remember, they used to put on delightful humoresques, but there was some serious acting too. Correct me if I'm wrong."

"You're not wrong. At one time we had a proper classical repertoire. The theater has changed since then, of course."

"A holiday of sorts, I understand."

"In a sense. If you can call being fired from your job a holiday. I have no regrets. I've learned to have no regrets."

"You have my heartfelt respect," said the man with Old World courtesy.

He looked about fifty. His suit was of the old-fashioned cut, not new but very well preserved. He may have been a bank clerk, or perhaps a tutor to the sons of the rich.

"Engel is my name. Permit me to invite you to join me in a cup of coffee. I have a thermos flask. I would never have imagined how useful that little gadget would prove to be in this place. Without coffee and cigarettes I can't get through the day. The hatch is opened and shut according to the caprices of the cook."

"A moment," said Lotte. "Be so kind as to wait for me a moment."

She stood in front of the mirror and made up her face. Over the years she had invested much labor in this face. It had changed, grown ravaged, the neck, the eye holes. Her late mother had been fond of saying that maturity too had a beauty of its own. How she hated those old saws. Adding insult to injury. If not for her face, her career would have been different. Beautiful woman always got to the top in the end. She suffered especially on account of her ears, which seemed to her too long and prominent. And in recent years, her hair. It was falling out at a horrifying rate. And dyeing it only emphasized its sparseness. The time she spent in front of the mirror making up her face was always one of stocktaking and soul-searching. At these moments generalizations hardened in her brain like needles. Now she felt her reflections gathering into a point again. She finished quickly, stepped outside, and announced: "I'm ready."

"We men are billeted on the ground floor, but as long as we have our thermos flask life's not as bad as it seems." The time Lotte had spent in front of the mirror with her makeup had relaxed her facial muscles. She felt a sense of relief.

The room was full of books, reminding her of her father's room at home. Her father was addicted to books like other men are to alcohol. What little money he had he spent on buying books. In the remote provincial backwater books were expensive, and he wasted half his salary on them. Right up to the end her mother reproached her dead husband for this sin. Immediately after his death, her mother had sold his books for a pittance to a Jew with a skullcap who came from Vienna with a van. Lotte remembered the empty room with its insides ripped out.

"The coffee may not look like anything special, but it's hot, if I may be permitted to say something in its praise."

"I find it delicious," said Lotte. "By the way, what does one do here? Is there a program?"

A look of surprise crossed the man's face and he said, "I play the violin. Three or four hours a day, for the time being. I can't say that I have improved. Improvement on an instrument like the violin is no easy matter."

"Nevertheless."

"My dear lady, I have made great efforts over the years. The will exists, but that one little defect makes any real progress impossible."

"What defect are you speaking of?"

"Internal, in the main. The great Sebastian, with whom I studied, even succeeded in locating it exactly. It's the shoulder, the right shoulder upsets the balance, and with it the sound and all that implies."

"Strange," said Lotte. She was still thirsty.

"The defect is essentially hereditary, that's why I was so glad when I was invited to come here and eradicate it for once and for all. The rest of the time I spend in exercise."

"A kind of refresher course, in other words."

"You might say so. The truth of the matter is that I was dismissed from my job. I don't blame them. When all is said and done, you can't hide a defect for ever."

34

"Did you ever happen to come across Manfred Shtorch?"

Engel opened his eyes wide and said, "A childhood friend. We went to school together, at the liberal arts high school, and after that we both studied with the same violin teacher. I haven't seen him for years. I hear he's gone over to the viola. A gifted man."

"My ex-husband," said Lotte.

"Forgive me," said Engel, as if he had touched a hidden wound. "It's been years since I saw him. At school we were very friendly. He was brilliant, not only at music. He sat in the second row, at the desk in front of mine. Please forgive me," he adeed, as if he had been burned again.

Lotte suddenly felt as if her former life, full of action, frenzy and excitement, had stopped clamoring inside her. She lowered her head, as she always did when she was faced with a decision which was beyond her strength.

"The grant is very generous, and enables me to devote myself completely to the violin. I'm not sure if it's possible to eradicate hereditary defects. The gymnastics appear to be beneficial, but hardly sufficient, it seems to me, to eradicate defects. They are great believers in gymnastics here."

"On the contrary," said Lotte, scarcely aware of the words coming out of her mouth. "On the contrary. Improvement is possible, perfection is possible."

35

"Is it really?" asked the man in surprise.

"Of course it is. I believe in will power. Where there's a will there's a way."

Engel bowed his head, like a man whose error has been exposed.

"Reform is possible. Of course it's possible. Anything is possible. All you need is the will, and that we have in full measure." All at once she sensed that she was talking as if she had been drinking brandy. It was the weariness, the fatigue of the past few weeks, which had spread through all her limbs. "I'm dying for the long vacation," she said, "but before that I need a rest, long vacations require long rests, if I may put it that way."

"I understand. No one comes here the easy way. And everything is different here, including the climate. I myself slept the whole day."

"I'm glad," said Lotte absentmindedly. "A wonderful holiday. My work over the past few years has worn me out. I need a long, deep vacation in order to get back on my feet and begin again. It's possible to begin again; if only there's a will it's possible to begin again."

"It's possible to recuperate here." The man echoed her words.

"In that case, let us begin right away," said Lotte, and rose to her feet.

"Permit me to escort you to your room. Sleep here, as you will see for yourself, is wonderful." He spoke to her the way the family doctor, Dr. Lachan, used to speak when examining her as a child. He too was a short, thin man. "Straight ahead, straight ahead," he said. "Up the stairs and here we are. Room number thirty-seven, if I'm not mistaken." But to Lotte it seemed, for some reason, that he was talking not to her but to himself.

FOUR

That whole day she slept and when she woke the light was already streaming through the window again. She remembered that she had wandered very far inside herself. She did not remember where. Her sleep was heavy and she swam in it as in a thick liquid. Now she extricated herself and sat up in bed. The room was bare of decoration. On the shelf were a few bottles of makeup, a couple of books and a pair of scissors: in other words, a woman had lived here before her.

She wiped the sweat off her forehead. This act, as if by magic, conjured up her daughter's face, a face heavy with sorrow. After her marriage to George her hands had lost their freedom and she had begun to stand like a muzzled animal. Now, for the first time in years, Lotte felt a kind of closeness to her. She wanted to embrace her and press her swollen hands to her heart.

There was a commotion in the passage again. An elegantly dressed woman, no longer young, stood next to the hatch and set forth her complaints in fluent, urban German without the faintest taint of a foreign accent. The arrangements in this place were driving her out of her mind. She could no longer endure the muddle. Herbert stood beside her, tall and embarrassed, and tried to pacify her: it was only the cook. A woman with no manners, she would be taught a lesson. He spoke in a quiet, matter-of-fact tone. But the woman was firm, she refused to accept his explanations. All the arrangements here were chaotic. For some reason, she called them disgracefully Jewish arrangements. "On no account am I prepared to go on staying here," she said, as if she were addressing the proprietor of a hotel whose establishment had been found wanting.

Herbert, who did not leave her side and appeared to understand her anger, announced firmly: "Order will be restored." This sentence made an impression on the woman. She passed her right hand over her brow, as if she were exhausted after some strenuous effort, took a step backward, and stopped. Herbert, who appeared deeply appreciative of this gesture, said, "The Director of the Institute will be notified of this immediately," and escorted her elegantly from the scene of the fire.

The woman, whose posture was now very erect, walked straight into the hall. The faces of the people standing around the hatch expressed satisfaction. It was hard to tell what it was, exactly, that had aroused their admiration: Herbert's powers of persuasion or the woman's resolute stand. The uproar, in any case, calmed down.

A few coffee pots and slices of bread smeared with jam lay scattered about on the tables. The sight made Lotte think of a hasty meal in an army barracks. But she was very thirsty and she overcame her disgust. The lukewarm coffee slid down her gullet and caused her pain. In the last few months her ulcer had come to life again. Ever since she was a child her digestive organs had given her trouble. After she separated from her husband the pains suddenly subsided, but in the last few years they had revived again, flooding her in wave after wave, like gusts of rage. In the end they had discovered the ulcer. When the doctors informed her of the diagnosis she burst into tears. That was seven years ago. Many storms had raged over her head since then. She made up her mind: no one would discover her secret. And while she was standing there a voice was heard in the hall. The affair, it appeared, was not yet over. The woman sat on the armchair speaking quietly but distinctly: "What am I doing here? These Jewish arrangements. They

don't even give you a cup of coffee in the morning."
Vestiges of beauty were still apparent on her face.
Her clothes too were full of simple elegance. There
was no one next to her and she was giving vent to
her feelings with a quiet bitterness. Herbert appeared at the side door and immediately informed
her: "I've just spoken to the Director of the Institute.
He promised to reprimand her. Tomorrow the
hatch will be open till nine o'clock."

"He's already promised once." The woman was
not appeased.

"This time he promised solemnly."

The woman raised her head and with a gesture
full of disdain she said, "I don't believe in the sol-
emn promises of these people."

"You don't say so."

"These Jews, all they can think about is money.
Their meanness drives them out of their minds."

"As for me," said Herbert calmly and deliberately, "I'd be inclined to wait and see."

"My patience is at an end," she said shortly.

Herbert knew that the time for words and arguments was now past. His long, pale face grew somewhat anxious. No one came to his assistance. The
sharp words stood in the air. Lotte took a few steps
toward Herbert. "Do you remember me?" This was
the way she would always approach close friends
she had not seen for years, with a kind of demon-
strative self-confidence. And Herbert, preoccupied
with his own little worry, said absentmindedly,

"Lotte Schloss. Who could forget. Allow me to introduce Lotte Schloss." He turned to the seated woman.

"Isadora Rotenberg," said the woman with deliberate dryness.

"We are discussing a very weighty matter," said Herbert.

"What can it be," wondered Lotte.

"Our cook. The controversy has already been raging for a month. From when to when should the hatch be open for morning coffee? A whole theology has been constructed around this point by the cook."

"How admirable of her," said Lotte with affected gravity.

"The hussy," hissed Isadora.

"Who is she?" asked Lotte in a whisper.

"A woman who is not content to be a cook, but who harbors pedagogical ambitions as well. She wants to teach us punctuality, order and what she refers to as self-discipline. Thank goodness her sphere of influence is but a narrow one, thank goodness it's only the hatch. Otherwise she would have made our lives a hell on earth."

"You call the hatch a narrow sphere of influence, sir? You call our morning coffee a narrow sphere? If that's a narrow sphere I'd like to know what a broad one is. Perhaps you would be so good as to explain it to me."

Herbert's face lost its gravity in an instant and he

42

burst out laughing. "I beg your pardon. The hatch is not a narrow sphere, not by any means."

Isadora did not move a muscle. She pursued her lips as if in anticipation of some new argument. But no new argument was advanced.

"Are you too a member of our race?" Isadora turned to Lotte, addressing her in the tone of an older woman condescending to a younger one.

"I am."

"You are in store for some surprises here."

"I'm ready," said Lotte, and opened both her arms.

"Miss Schloss is an actress by profession," said Herbert.

"What is an actress doing in this graveyard?" said Isadora, without blinking an eye.

"I," said Lotte, "have learned to have no regrets."

"So, we still have something to learn," said Isadora to Herbert, not without a trace of irony.

FIVE

In the afternoon Lotte went out for a walk. Some compelling desire drew her outside. It was full daylight and a deep calm lay over the dense forests. I must go out, she said to herself, as she used to say in days gone by, when the company was touring the remote mountain villages. It was different now. Just how different, she was yet to learn. In any case, the burden dropped from her shoulders and she felt relief, as after an exhausting journey.

For some reason she remembered the resorts she used to visit with her parents during the summer holidays. They stayed in seedy pensions where the food was gray and elderly Jews in black skullcaps haunted the corridors like ghosts. Her father would have preferred to stay at home with his beloved books, but as soon as summer arrived her mother, tormented by hidden desires, would begin to fill the house with an evil spirit, a restless wanderlust. She must get out, get out at any cost. There was no money; they had to take her gold necklace to the pawnshop. This shameful expedition did not pass off without recriminations, complaints and abuse. In the end they set out, in the hope that this time the pension would be respectable, clean, that coffee would be served in the afternoon, the band would play waltzes and the guests would speak proper German. Disappointment soon followed. Resigned to their fate, they took two narrow rooms in one of the cramped pensions where a few textile merchants, smugglers and moneychangers lurked in the passage. After one day's stay the fraud was exposed in all its nakedness: the food was inedible, the mattresses filthy and in the afternoon children ran up and down the corridors as if the place were an orphanage. Her mother, beside herself with rage, would pounce on the janitor and upbraid him. And in the end, after an exchange of threats, they would leave. It was the same every summer, ever since the distant days of her early childhood. Her father was a quiet, withdrawn man, who never said, I told you so. But her mother, afraid of hearing just these words, would get in first and attack him viciously. His books. All their money had been wasted on books.

Her mother had invested all her love in her. Her

45

father's presence was not felt in the house. From year to year he secluded himself more and more in his room, a narrow room filled with books. He worked long hours as a clerk in a department store, and when he came home at night he would bury himself in his narrow room, emerging only to make himself a cup of tea. Lotte could not remember even one look of his, but many years later, in some remote inn, she met a woman, a Jewess as it transpired, who had known her father well in Transylvania, in the town of his birth where he had been regarded as a genius in his youth, and where at the age of sixteen he had published a booklet which had made a great stir. This simple woman spoke about her father as if he were a saint, cut off from his origins due to some terrible mistake.

After the performance was over they sat together all night long. The woman had talked and she had listened. There was a strange serenity in her voice. Lotte said to herself: One day I'll go to my father's birthplace, to Marmoresh. But it was only a passing thought. The tours devoured her time. Her mother, who lived to a ripe old age, never mentioned her father except when speaking of the rundown house, the shabby furniture and the constant hardships of her life. But her love for her daughter was boundless. She was sure that it was only because she had not given her enough clothes, enough money, that she had not reached the top. All her daughter's eccentricities, and they were many, she interpreted in a favorable light. Strangely enough, Lotte did not feel much love for her in return. When she fell on hard times she would go home to her, not to talk but to eat a home-cooked meal. When she graduated from high school and entered the acting academy her mother's joy knew no bounds. She bought a new dress and went out to buy furniture for the house. She had no money, of course, but her pride, after all the years of humiliation, took a new lease on life. The neighbors, of course, saw things differently: delusions of grandeur had made her lose her wits. The thought that her only daughter had been accepted by the acting academy, and even been awarded a partial grant, nourished her dreams for many years to come. And once, when the grocer refused to give her bread on credit, she did not curb her tongue and said, "You will not be invited to the opening night."

It did not take long for Lotte to get into trouble. One of the directors, a man without morals, seduced her and she allowed herself to be seduced. She imagined in her innocence that her lover would stand by his promises and marry her, but the moment he heard that she was pregnant he scowled and shouted, "Damn it all!" Lotte wept. In the end, in order to console her, he said, "Believe me, it's nothing. All the girls have been to the gynecologist. He's a Jew, he'll do anything for money."

The next morning she was already sitting in the waiting room. The doctor, a short man with a horribly Jewish face, examined her and said, "Girls your age should be careful. We'll do what has to be done." This sentence, steeped in a smell of drugs and disinfectant, she would never forget. In an instant her youth lay trampled sordidly underfoot. She went on studying diligently and resolutely. She did not visit her mother often. Her mother went short in order to send her part of her pension every month. These banknotes too, which reached her every month by registered post, wrapped up in newspaper, she would never forget.

At about this time the first, bitter lines began to appear on her face, and soon her neck too was ringed with lines. When she first discovered these lines, a girl of twenty-one years old, she sank into despair. The next day she made up her mind: Come what may, I shall never betray my mother's dreams.

That winter her mother died. One of the neighbors sent her a telegram. When she arrived the next day the house was already standing empty. The funeral, it transpired, had taken place the evening before. At the offices of the Jewish congregation nobody knew the reason for this indecent haste. One of the clerks, a coarse-natured fellow, said casually, "We didn't know if you were coming." Lotte, who had intended making a scene, froze in her place.

The following days were shockingly practical. She paid the death duties, the municipal taxes and the grocery bills. The house with all it contained she sold to a Jewish dealer. Of all that cold commotion she remembered only the red face of the dealer. He paid in cash.

She graduated from the academy with distinction and immediately began work in a cabaret. She had a pleasant voice, clear pronunciation and no mean dramatic talent. Not long afterward she found work in the theater.

She married Manfred at the age of twenty-three. He was a man with no distinguishing features, bald and bespectacled. He looked like a grocer or a doorman. Of one thing she was sure: he would not come between her and her career. And in fact, no sooner were they married than her ambition rose to new heights. She worked on every small part with grim determination. Manfred did not stand in her way. He cooked dinner himself. Sometimes she was away from home for weeks on end. On her return he would ask no more than was absolutely necessary. His kindness, to tell the truth, maddened her. He was a gentle man by nature.

Julia was born and brought her no joy. Manfred asked for leave and looked after the baby. Lotte took off on a tour with the company. When his leave was over Manfred hired an old woman to take care of the child. Lotte came back from her travels exhausted. Manfred asked few questions, spent hours practicing in the basement.

And thus the days passed. Each of them went about his or her own affairs. Sometimes Manfred too went on tour with the orchestra. His trips were for the most part short and he always came back on time. Later on, when she felt that her career was in danger of failing, she yelled at Manfred, but Manfred never yelled back.

The separation brought her sudden relief. When she heard that Manfred had gone east, to the town of his birth, she felt no anger. The thought that Julia would now be exclusively hers made her very happy.

When she discovered her own style on the stage, it was already too late. She was nearly forty, one of many actresses playing minor roles. In vain she tried to put up a fight. One after the other younger performers came to the forefront and she was pushed aside.

In the spring of 1937 it was already clear that her days in the theater were coming to an end. She was the only Jewess in the company. Nevertheless, they spoke of the Jews who were taking over the theater and not giving the younger generation a chance. She fought, wrote letters and called on old friends for help. One after the other the doors were closed in her face. The letter of dismissal came in the post. The reason given was a breach of solidarity. It was as if her thirty years in the theater had never existed.

For two days she shut herself up in her room, drinking coffee and smoking cigarettes. Immediately afterward, defeated and exhausted, she got on a train and went to her daughter.

George did not like her. As a middle-class Austrian he disliked independent women. He was a man of limited education and the sophisticated city words his mother-in-law bandied about the house embarrassed him. At first he said little and examined her suspiciously. Later on, he said that the theater corrupted the youth. What was the theater, when all was said and done, but a lot of half-naked women and the kind of language decent people would never use. He was not a religious man, but on Sundays he went to church. When his sons grew up he took them with him so that they would learn how to behave themselves. The boys resembled their father, healthy and dull. In the evening, when he came home from work, he cast fear into the hearts of his family. And on Saturday night, like every respectable Austrian, he came home drunk.

She was looking for a refuge and she found a hell. What wasn't said and what wasn't shouted! She soon realized that not only her friends but even her family, her last resort, all of them, her only daughter too, had turned their backs on her. In the end, with no other choice, she announced in the voice of a person announcing his own suicide: If nobody wants me any more—I'll go to the Jews.

51

SIX

She walked down the hill, and the pictures pursued her like jumbled scenes from a movie. Each picture with its own fiasco, but above all, the dark offices in which she had stood and asked for help. Nobody wanted to help her, not even her so-called friends. Since nobody came forward to help her, she and Julia hurried up and down the streets. The spring sunlight poured down from the sky and the trees on the pavements were in full blossom. All that simple and familiar loveliness only cast her deeper into despair.

She did not hurry now. She passed from path to path, pausing from time to time to lean against a tree. In the light of the sinking day there was a kind of melancholy sweetness whose like she had not experienced for many years. She was not afraid. Her steps grew shorter, more careful. As if she wanted to draw the hour out and make it last.

And as she stood leaning against the trunk of a tree, she noticed a little sign made of wood. She approached and read: "On this spot our friend, our sister in spirit, Sophia Traube, took her own life. 15.6.1937." Lotte, who had been about to bend down, recoiled. She looked again: a board nailed to a narrow strip of wood planted in the ground. The writing was neat, but plain. It was evident that the hand that had written these words had done so with great care. "There must be some mistake," she said out loud, as if to dispel some frightening shadow.

Then she stood up straight and threw back her hair. This gesture, which she had affected since her high school days, always revived her and brought to mind a phrase or an idea. But now it seemed to turn her temples to ice. Fear sent cold shivers down her spine.

She began to climb back up the hill. She strayed from the path and grasped at branches growing low on the trees. The gently fading daylight suddenly turned gray. She began to hurry, and the more she hurried the farther she strayed.

When she reached the building at last the sky was already dark. Next to the hatch people were standing in a queue, their tin bowls in their hands. They stood still, without exchanging a word. And through the glass of the dividing door they looked sunk in contemplation. When she recognized Herbert, she was emboldened to open the door.

"Where is the ritual bowl," said Herbert without formality.

"Upstairs. I'll run and get it." She recovered her voice, and it sounded surprisingly young.

"Time will soon be up. Another ten minutes."

Her calf muscles were cramped from running up the hill, but she made the effort, not without a vigorous grace, as if she were running too close an open door in winter, so that the cold wind would not burst into the house.

In less than a minute she was standing in the queue, the tin bowl and cutlery in her right hand, the mug in her left. "I'm ready," she said. Herbert straightened his shoulders like a soldier in the reserves, whose temporary service in the army showed that the marrow had not yet dried up in his bones.

The cook took the two bowls and placed in each a potato in its skin, a piece of fish, and a slice of beetroot. Herbert took the two bowls and when they reached the table he gave one of them to Lotte. "Something new today," he announced. "The color red has made its appearance among us again." Next to them people ate silently. Every now and then a complaint made itself heard from the sidelines.

Herbert looked satisfied. The dense color of the beetroot brought a jovial twinkle to his eye.

There were a number of latecomers, of course. They stood next to the hatch, despairing or bitterly amused, among them two men dressed with simple elegance. They looked like a couple of department heads whose instructions had not been carried out. Only the tin bowls bore witness to a different status. One of them approached the hatch and tapped on it with the cry: "Two minutes late. Will even they be counted against us?" His cry was not answered. Afterward they sat down beside their empty bowls.

Lotte asked, "Did you know Sophia Traube?"

"What a question." Herbert raised his eyes. "I sat next to her as I'm sitting next to you now. Who could have guessed." His modest happiness clouded. "A poetic soul, without any exaggeration. We tried, how shall I put it, to draw her in, but Sophia was devoured by her own longings. She could not reconcile herself."

"And did no one come to visit her?"

"No, unfortunately not."

Lotte regretted having darkened Herbert's modest joy. Although he went on eating, his face remained despondent.

"Forgive me," said Lotte.

The meal was coming to an end. A few people stood by the long sink and washed their dishes. The sight reminded Lotte of the yard of an army camp, but she immediately realized her mistake. These people were no longer young, well-dressed, their movements too were restrained and subdued, and showed consideration for each other's privacy. "There's no hot water," said one of them. There was no tone of exaggeration to his complaint. He stood to one side and dried his bowl and cutlery with a white cloth.

Isadora sat in the armchair. She had taken no part in the hurried meal. Herbert approached her, bowed, and asked, "What's wrong?"

"Nothing. Fried fish is not enough to get me out of my chair."

"Beetroot," said Herbert.

"Beetroot reminds me of the cook's face."

"Do not, I beg you," said Herbert pompously, "desecrate that wine-red, Dionysian color."

Isadora laughed.

The meal came noiselessly to its end. And for a moment the place seemed like a country hostel, where no one paid much attention to etiquette.

"What I miss most is a good cigar," someone whispered in Herbert's ear, as if confessing a weakness.

"Haven't they sent you any?"

"Unfortunately not," said the man, and turned away.

And as the darkness gathered at the windows they began to prepare for the nightly games. Some of them brought the chessmen and placed them on the boards. It was evident that they had been waiting for this moment for many hours.

"How do you find our little retreat?" a man approached her and asked.

"Charming," said Lotte absent mindedly.

SEVEN

And one by one the days passed by. Lotte rose early
in the morning and went out immediately to walk
around the mountain. The last days of summer
were fine, mild and flawless. The evenings were
fresh and cool. Little by little the sights dropped
away, not all at once and not entirely, but they no
longer disturbed her as they had done at first. I'm
on holiday, she would say when a sudden memory
pounced on her. But her nights were troubled. At
night the old terrors ruled her without restraint.
She would wake in the middle of a nightmare and
not be able to fall asleep again till dawn.

And thus the month of September passed. In the
month of October her heart told her that Julia
would come to visit her. For several days she kept
close to the building and waited for her at the door,

but when she did not come she stopped expecting her. But Isadora was not forgotten. She received a big parcel full of goodies: boxes of chocolates, coffee, cigarettes, English tea and dates. They were all happy, but not Isadora. She spread these luxuries out in front of everyone and announced: "Take whatever you wish." And thus she gave expression to her disgust with the charity sent her by her daughters.

It was a long time since the inmates of the retreat had set eyes on such luxuries. They were happy and made jokes. Once more they began to talk about the plain. About the bustling cities, the cafés and restaurants. Isadora did not react, save for a couple of cutting remarks.

And in the midst of the happiness and excitement, a tall man with the air of an independent farmer appeared at the back door.

Everyone fell silent. "Come in," said Isadore. "Allow me to offer you some of the delicacies sent us from the plains."

"You want to corrupt me too, then."

"Do such insignificant luxuries have the power to corrupt?"

"One sin leads to another, as I've always said," pronounced the man in a bucolic voice. "Today Swiss chocolate and tomorrow tidbits of cheese and the body which I have worked so hard to cure will be beyond redemption again, as hopelessly Jewish as it was in the beginning."

"I see we are back on the old subject again," said Isadora nastily.

"We are not at liberty to ignore it."

"Nobody can call me a Jewess. I have nothing in common with them."

"I'm not so sure," said the man in a milder tone.

"You can still doubt it."

"I'm a simple man," he said humbly. "My education is as small as a grain of wheat. Most of my life was spent with horses. It was from them I learned the virtues of nature."

"Nature," interrupted Isadora, and pulled a face.

"The Jews are hated by all, a fact I think nobody can deny."

"Yes, because they are Jews."

"And you, madam, are quite untainted by them."

"Yes."

"Let others be the judge of that," said the man in the tone of a farmer engaged upon a quarrel.

"I am my own judge."

The tall, strong-looking man suddenly appeared ill at ease, as if the circumstances were too much for him. He leaned his hand on the table and hung his head. His confidence seemed to have evaporated.

"Nobody will tell me who or what I am any more, nobody," insisted Isadora.

At the sound of these last words a broad, gentle smile spread over the man's bucolic face and he said, "I'm not saying a word."

"In that case, why don't you stop preaching."

"I wasn't preaching. All I was trying to do was teach you the lessons of nature, the virtues of the horse, the benefits of a healthy diet, the cunning of the hunter, the pleasures of sport, of wine. It has nothing to do with preaching. I'm not a preacher, I'm a simple horse farmer. I saw the suffering of my race and I wanted to share my experience with them. My experience, madam, is considerable."

"But we, sir, are not animals."

"And nevertheless, madam, nevertheless . . ." He searched for words and could not find them. He raised his head with the air of a baffled peasant and clung desperately to the table.

At this moment it seemed that someone must rise to his feet and extend a helping hand to this strong man in his great confusion and embarrassment. But no one rose. They all sat still in their places as if they were taking part in a play.

"Who is that man?" asked Lotte in a whisper.

"That is Balaban, the great Balaban."

In the meantime the man turned his back on them. The door closed soundlessly behind him.

Later Herbert told her the story. Balaban was a Jew, a horse trader by profession. Seven years ago he had bought this place from the Jewish-Christian Friendship League, which used to hold monthly seminars there, with the intention of converting it into a sanatorium. He conducted an investigation and concluded that there were about fifty aging Jews in the district, in good health and with private means, who were a burden to their children. It began as a commercial venture, so to say, but then things grew more complicated. Balaban put out a glossy, confidence-inspiring prospectus and distributed it all over the district. In this prospectus he offered mountain air, medical supervision, peace of mind and a kosher kitchen. His calculations were thorough, but not accurate. The last-mentioned attraction gave rise to the suspicion that he was advertising a Jewish old age home. Balaban took note of his mistake and learned his lesson. A year later he brought out a different prospectus in a different color, with no mention of the shameful dietary detail and, above all, with an entirely different program: horseback riding, swimming, seasonal hunting, organized hikes and what he called assimilation into the countryside. This proposal was well received by all. Balaban promised that within a short space of time he would painlessly eradicate embarrassing Jewish gestures and ugly accents. No one would have to be ashamed any more.

He himself, by the way, was originally from a small village in Poland. He arrived in the district after the First World War when he was only twenty years old. In spite of his youth he had already made up his mind: no more infirmity of spirit. And the results spoke for themselves. He began his life here as a stable boy, and before long he knew how to look after a horse as well as the most experienced groom on the estate. Three or four years later he owned a stable and horses of his own. His affairs prospered and he invested his profits, like the other natives of the place, in land. He had bought the retreat for a song, and it was here that his troubles began.

In the first year the experiment seemed to be succeeding. The residents began their day with a run, they rode horses, played tennis, ate yogurt and learned to drink wine. Balaban himself guided them in their new way of life.

But the venture upon which he had embarked as a commercial enterprise captured his imagination. He neglected his other, prosperous affairs, and devoted himself completely to his new vocation—to turn the sickly members of his race into a healthy breed. True, some of them could not stand the grueling pace and left, but others persevered. After a year of labor they went back to town changed and full of health. Some said that in the first year he had treated the residents harshly, and some still remembered him from those early days and told stories about him, not without admiration.

But complications set in due to certain mistakes, muddles and misunderstandings. Balaban, who shied away from explaining his ideas in words, got dragged against his will into arguments, began to smoke, play cards and put on weight. His big face, once ruddy with health, grew flabby, and some of the old gestures which he had pulled out by the roots as a young man came back to vex him.

63

"Now he's just like one of us, even weaker than we are. From time to time he speaks of going down to the village in order to recover his strength. That, madam, is the story. Food for thought, madam."

Lotte stirred. The account, although many of its details were not quite clear, moved her. There were many questions she would have liked to have asked, but she did not know where to begin. She felt a delicate sadness for this Balaban whose dreams had come to nothing.

Afterward they sat drinking coffee and smoking and watched the people sitting round the tables avidly playing cards.

EIGHT

The next morning Lotte woke up early and discovered to her delight that the bath taps were working and, what was more, the water was hot. In an instant she shook off her drowsiness and removed her clothes, and while the water was running and filling the bath she managed to subject her naked body to a hurried scrutiny. Her body, her secret home, had changed unrecognizably over the past year. She had followed these changes anxiously and tried to cover up the cracks gaping in the exposed parts of her body. The thought that her body was wearing out preyed on her mind.

Now the secret ravages were exposed in all their nakedness. Her flesh fell loosely about her, as if it had come undone from its moorings. Even her an-

65

kles, her only beauty, were swollen. Her legs stood on the cold floor, heavy and cylindrical.

The hot, soft water enveloped her instantly and wiped the anxiety momentarily from her heart. She drowned in the water with her eyes closed. She lay soaking for a long time and as her body soaked her senses quickened and revived. No longer thoughts but pictures, pleasant pictures from her many travels.

There were times, not so long ago, when she still believed that her tired body would find a resting place by the side of some simple man in a remote cottage where the bread was fresh and warm, vegetables grew outside the windows, horses grazed in the meadow and the fences were covered with creepers. From her youth she had been drawn, probably because of the literature she read, to these wild outposts of nature, and sometimes when the company toured the mountain regions she would say to herself: I'll stay here. The man loves me. What do I care about the theater?

But the simple men were not so simple. They had ideas of their own, crudities of their own, and in bed they treated a woman like a household cat. Nature was not innocent, it appeared, it had perversities of its own. Although she knew this, she would allow herself to be seduced by her old beliefs again. When Julia married George she had been glad to think that she, at least, would be happy. But George, so blond and healthy looking in his youth, an offshoot of the local peasant stock, and innocent as far as the eye could see, proved no different from any other Austrian: coarse, lustful and eaten up with envy.

She wrapped herself in the big, thick towel which she took with her wherever she went. If there was anything in the world which gave her constant pleasure, it was this soft piece of cloth. And she in turn felt true affection for it, as if it were a domestic pet. This cotton towel, which she had purchased from an old peasant woman in a remote village, had a magic power to pull her out of the mire of her thoughts and bring her back to life.

After soaking for almost an hour she discovered to her surprise that her tired body, which only an hour ago had resembled a lump of dough, had re-covered its shape. This modest joy was unlike any other.

She had missed breakfast, of course, and Herbert was unable to offer her even a tepid cup of coffee from his thermos flask.

"Why don't we go and sit in a café," she said, but no sooner were the words out of her mouth then she realized her mistake. There were no cafés here for miles around. Here there were only trees, and what-ever could be derived from trees.

Besides Lotte there were a number of others standing around the hatch, waiting for the favors of the cook and the miracle that never materialized. No one came out to serve them. "Isn't there any-thing at all?" said Lotte with a hungry smile.

"We'll try our charms on the kitchen maid," said

Herbert, and immediately disappeared from view.

And he was as true as his word. After coaxing and cajoling the kitchen maid and pulling the wool over the eyes of the cook, he emerged with a pot of coffee and a few slices of bread and jam piled on a plate. Lotte welcomed him like a conquering hero bearing trophies and they all applauded happily. Isadora, who was sitting in the corner watching Herbert's escapades with a hint of envy, did not curb her tongue, and whispered, "Open doors invite a thief." Lotte's participation in this little adventure revived in her, as if by magic, a strong sense of life. The tepid coffee suddenly tasted delicious.

Herbert, in high spirits, told her the kitchen maid's story in an imitation of the local idiom. She was a farmer's daughter, it transpired, born in the mountains, who served Balaban as a living model for training the Jews in the wisdom of the senses. He had found her in the mountains and presented her forthwith to the inmates as a jewel of nature—a jewel, moreover, who knew how to prepare good food untainted by the corruption of the city: yogurt and cheese. Now all that remained to her was a little peasant cunning—she would sell you her household gods for flattery and a small bribe.

Herbert was happy and in his happiness he announced: "A little bribery will get you whatever you want."

"But I have no money, my dear," confessed Lotte.

"Never mind. A little charm will do the trick instead. A wave of our magic wand. Logic gave up the ghost in this place a long time ago."

They sat outside. The light was cold, the surrounding slopes spread their arms, bare and leafless, in a wide embrace. The shades of autumn were everywhere. Every now and then the leaves, remnant of its glory, rose a little from the earth, as if in one last attempt to rise from the dead.

"Is there a program here?" asked Lotte.

"Of course, but it's veiled in mystery. All the best things are veiled in mystery."

"What is your surname, if I may ask," it suddenly occurred to her to inquire.

"Zuntz."

"Herbert Zuntz, the journalist?"

"No other. The former journalist."

"How wonderful," said Lotte, as if she were seeing him for the first time.

Two years before he had been fired from the editorial board of *Der Tag* with no reason and no severance pay. Friends, connections, rights and personal charms, all were of no avail. For a year he fought, and then with nowhere else to go and on the brink of despair he found his way here, to the mountains and Balaban.

Herbert Zuntz, one of the illustrious names of Austrian journalism, the pupil and disciple of Karl Kraus. Like his teacher he too fought the evils of the time, the corruption of morals and language. In the course of the years he had made a number of enemies, and they did not miss their opportunity when it came. When the time was ripe, they fired him.

Herbert did not refer to his days of fame by so much as a single word. His open eyes shone with a mild irony which no longer wished to warn or sting, but seemed content to look inward. When he mentioned his home even this hint of irony disappeared and a delicate sadness flooded his eyes.

"Our children will no longer suffer," Lotte hastened to console him.

"Probably not."

"Although, in my heart of hearts I must confess, these Austrian farmers are not my type."

Herbert seemed to know exactly what she was hinting at. He bowed his gray head like a man whose wounds had been exposed to a cold wind.

"These farmers, who once seemed to us so innocent and naïve, are no different from the common workingman," she said emphatically.

That evening Balaban appeared in the hall again. He sat down next to one of the tables and observed the poker game. He might have been a farmer who had lost his land or a Jewish speculator. His face was thick and unshaven. He too, apparently, was excited by the game. But every now and then he seemed to lose interest, and closed his eyes. And then it seemed that some inner anxiety was forcing him to withdraw into himself.

"The great Balaban," said Lotte in astonishment.

Once or twice he rose from his seat as if about to leave the hall on some urgent errand. But it was only an illusion. He was only standing up in order to approach some other table, where the stakes were higher. Only two years ago poker had been absolutely forbidden. Balaban was of the opinion that poker was a Jewish disease which had to be pulled up by the roots. Billiards, on the other hand, he permitted, as being more of a sport. Now the billiard table stood deserted in the next room. The people played cards to their heart's desire, until late at night, until intoxication and total exhaustion.

"Permit me to introduce Miss Lotte Schloss." Herbert turned to Balaban. "The well-known actress."

"Honored, I'm sure," said Balaban, in the tone of a hotel owner whose establishment may once have known better days, but which still maintained certain standards. "Have you shown the lady over our domain?"

"It will be done, it will be done," said Herbert.

Balaban spoke with the guttural local accent. And like a farmer who had acquired his education in the fields he got many words wrong. "Very glad to have you with us," he said. "We need some culture here." It was evident that the sphere to which he referred as "culture" was quite outside his ken. And indeed, he pronounced the word cautiously, as if he were afraid of touching it.

71

"I've explained everything to the lady already." Herbert came to his aid.

"I thank you from the bottom of my heart," said Balaban, as a man caught in a minefield might thank his rescuer.

NINE

The month of December was cold and gray and the rain fell without stopping. The inmates wrapped themselves in blankets and sat in the hall. The prohibition on speaking about the plain, which Balaban had imposed at the beginning, was still observed, like an old habit. A few people stood by the windows looking at the gray skies which promised nothing but more rain and cold.

From time to time Balaban appeared and apologized for his failure to get the heating working. The plumber who had promised to come had not arrived; as soon as the rain stopped he would go down to the village and fetch him himself. And indeed, every now and then Balaban did go down to the village. His affairs had gone from bad to worse. Ever since he had abandoned himself to his magic vision he had allowed all his other affairs to fall into neglect. Now he made jokes about the village, his affairs there, and himself. There was a certain bitterness about these jokes, but the inmates enjoyed listening to the rustic dialect and parables. In the end he always came back to the old complaint: the Jews could not be changed.

"Why?"

"Because they're Jews."

"What's wrong with that?"

"They're weak. The weak are always devoured in the end. That is the lesson of the countryside."

"What can they do about it?"

They could change. But the Jews would never change. They were pampered, sensitive, slow, argumentative.

Sometimes, when he was in a good humor, he would speak of his youth, his determination to become a horse trainer. How the horses had run away and how he had found them and brought them back. Once he had met a Jewish peddler and the Jew had taken fright and fled. Not at his appearance, but because he spoke to him in Yiddish.

But when he was in his cups he became gloomy. Angry with the world and everything in it, the Jews who refused to learn their lesson, the peasants who were stealing his property, himself and the kitchen maid who was wasting the food. His appearance changed too. His heavy, pockmarked face lost whatever gentleness it possessed and turned red, and he looked like an unruly peasant turned out of a bar. But even then no one was afraid of him. Herbert spoke to him tolerantly, humored him, and promised him that things would soon take a turn for the better. His stolen property would be returned to him and the thieves would be punished. And what about the Jews, he would demand, his sobriety returning. They too would come to their senses, Herbert would comfort him, they would learn their lesson and reform. He reminded him of Adolf Wolf, who had arrived in their midst two years before thin and stooped, looking just like a Jewish peddler. In the space of one year he had achieved the impossible. He had changed beyond recognition, he had even grown a mustache, and then he had returned to the plains.

And thus the days crept by. Exercise, someone would remember. Why aren't I exercising? Isn't that what I came here for? I left a flourishing shop, business connections, customers and friends. Instead of exercising, breathing fresh air into my lungs, I spend my time playing poker. Isn't that a crime! He forgot to mention a few insignificant details, of course: he had not abandoned his shop for nothing. The shop had gone downhill from one week to the next, his debtors had not paid their debts, his creditors had grown insistent, his friends had stopped visiting him, his good services to the village had been forgotten, his wife, the district nurse,

met her untimely death. The young men had persecuted him, throwing stones at his little shop as they
passed and shouting: Jews. He had come across
Balaban by chance, and Balaban had persuaded
him to come up to the mountain and change. He
had not wanted to come. In the end, lacking any
other choice, he had come.

He had come, but he had not fulfilled his obliga-
tions. He played poker as enthusiastically as if he
were a product of the city, sometimes too enthusiastically. When Balaban was in a bad mood he
would castigate him: "You've lived in the country.
You've seen trees and animals. And yet you've
learned nothing from them. Nothing. Why haven't
you learned?"

"They didn't teach me."

"Why didn't you look?"

"I did look."

"And why don't you know how to swim?"

"Nobody taught me."

"And what about horse riding, do you know how
to ride a horse?"

"No."

"So now do you understand why they broke your
windows?"

And when Balaban desisted and turned away, he
remained sitting in his chair and muttering to himself. "He's right of course. If I was stronger they
wouldn't have tormented me. All my troubles are
due to the fact that I have no determination, no

76

perseverance, I give up too soon. In short, I'm a coward."

Lotte too had lost her peace of mind. Two weeks before she had written a long letter to her daughter and expressed a wish to visit her. Her sins were not so great that she had to purge them in a convent. She missed the streets, the cafés, the theater. There was no reply. Herbert sat by her side and comforted her. He too received no letters. Nobody there received letters. That too was for the best.

"Who will pay for my stay here? Who will pay my fees?"

"Don't worry," said Herbert. "We will arrange a grant for you."

"A grant. How wonderful," said Lotte in a whisper.

For years this fantasy had haunted her imagination. A grant to go to Vienna. To Berlin. To be free for a year from the chains of the provincial theater, to see the world, breathe the atmosphere of true theater, great theater. Nothing, of course, came of these hopes. The grants were given to the young and promising, handsome young actors and, especially, pretty young actresses. Lotte was given small parts—shamefully, embarrassingly small. Small parts too, they told her, were important. And when she turned thirty they no longer said anything but "Take it or leave it, Lotte."

When the pretty, blank-faced actresses took liberties and skipped rehearsals, came late, didn't know their lines, said without shame, "I've forgotten, remind me," their self-indulgence was regarded as a charming caprice. Lotte hid her wounded pride and worked hard. Made something of nothing. True, from time to time she would be rewarded with a compliment, but for the most part nobody took any notice of her. The stars shone radiantly while she toiled obscurely in the wings, in a gray desert of anonymity.

"But how?" Lotte recovered her voice.

"It's quite simple. The board sits and makes its decisions. Believe me, they know what they're doing," said Herbert emphatically.

"But why me?" Her voice choked on the words.

"You were on the stage for years. As far as I know, you have never received a grant. Nobody ever bothered to ask, what is Lotte doing nowadays, or what have we done to advance Lotte. Small parts are important too, no doubt. But the time has come for greater things."

"But me, are you sure it's me," said Lotte, and there were tears in her eyes.

"Yes, you, you. Without a doubt, you. The board has been watching you for years. Nothing escapes their eyes. Justice is sometimes done in this world too."

Lotte felt uncomfortable. She wanted to escape to her room and cry. Supper brought her welcome relief. The hatch opened and the austere face of the cook appeared in its frame. Happiness such as she had not known for years flooded her. And as at the end of a play she wanted to curtsy and thank everybody. And later too, when she sat by herself in her room, the wave of warmth did not leave her. The thought that this time the board had noticed Lotte and chosen her, this thought momentarily stanched her hidden wound and she fell asleep as if she had swallowed a healing drug.

TEN

The next day it became known that Isadora had put an end to her life. The night before they had stayed up late playing cards as usual, although not excessively late. Isadora, as usual, took no part in the game, but she did not seem angry. She sat in the armchair and made a number of remarks about Balaban which were greeted with loud laughter. There was nothing unusual about this. And suddenly, silently, in the dark, without any warning, she had torn the thread of her life to shreds.

The woman who discovered the calamity stood leaning against the door, her hair rumpled and her staring eyes full of a cold terror. Nobody knew what to say. And as always after a shock the words welled up and burst out in all their nakedness. One small, shrill woman stood next to the eyewitness and muttered ceaselessly, "I told you, I told you." Her hollow words gave rise to no anger.

Nobody dared go into the room and confirm the bitter news. The hatch was open, but nobody wanted coffee. Herbert, for some reason, sat in the armchair. "She couldn't bear it," a woman pronounced. Strangely enough, this matter of fact sentence infuriated the eyewitness.

When Balaban appeared in the doorway he looked as if he had been dragged out of a deep sleep. His strong body and thick face were dull, heavy and disapproving. He went up to the door and knocked, and when there was no reply he went inside. A moment later he emerged. Any remaining hope was instantly crushed.

A dark quiet mingled with the faint smell of nocturnal perspiration invaded the corridor. People stood huddled in a circle a little way off. Balaban looked like an old peasant about to cross himself. Isadora lay on her bed, her long, fine face no longer expressing anything. A faint smile hovered at the corners of her lips.

The inmates retreated from the door and went into the lobby. The morning light had already crossed the glass door and lay on the floor, alternating with squares of shade. "That's life," said someone pointlessly.

"In ten minutes' time I'm closing the hatch," announced the cook—a warning that nobody needed.

No one had intended asking for breakfast. The shock was very deep. One or two people stood in a corner drinking coffee. They looked like petty thieves.

And in the shocked silence one or two people did not refrain from uttering long, pompous and somewhat indignant remarks, but nobody reacted and nobody argued. Their sorrow was very heavy. It absorbed the words as if they had not been spoken.

In the end Herbert was delegated to go inside and see if the dead woman had left any last request. Herbert put on his cap and went into the room with a strangely hurried step. The cook shut the hatch with a bang which sounded no different from usual.

It transpired that Isadore's last requests were to be buried without Jewish rites, that her daughters were not to be notified of her death and that no eulogies were to be delivered. These three negations now trembled in Herbert's hands. He read them aloud in a choked voice.

One after the other they gathered in the lobby. There were no more than twenty of them, and as they stood there huddled together they looked even less. And while they stood waiting, Balaban reappeared. Now he looked like a small-town Jewish laborer. As if the strong pagan lines had been wiped off his face. Balaban knew that the dead woman had not liked him, and this knowledge seemed to impose an extra obligation on him now. People seemed to understand this and no one expressed surprise at his presence. The eye witness, Mrs. Kron, asked to be left alone in the dead woman's room for a moment, and her request was granted.

Afterward everything became more organized. Herbert, Balaban and Mrs. Kron went down to the forest clearing and selected a suitable spot. The janitor brought a few spades and hoes up from the cellar. The crude, cylindrical implements seemed to show more than anything else what the nature of reality was.

When they returned from the forest Balaban's face was in utter confusion. He looked like a poor grave digger whose face had turned to earth with the labor of the years. His sorrow had no hope in it, only dumbness. The others stood next to the walls waiting for a sign. And when no signs was given they began smoking cigarettes. Before long the lobby was filled with dense smoke.

The funeral took place in the afternoon in the cold sunlight. The janitor wore his blue suit and tied a black band to his sleeve, thus giving public expression to their mourning. The others were dressed as usual. And although the dead woman had expressly requested no speeches to be made at her graveside, Herbert understood that it would be appropriate, and perhaps even to the liking of the departed, if a few of Rilke's poems were read. One thought led to another, and he asked Lotte to read.

Lotte was taken by surprise, and she pulled the little face of refusal she remembered from days gone by, when she was asked to stand in for another actor, but she immediately realized that this was not the appropriate expression now, and that it would be only right for her to accede to Herbert's modest request.

"Where is the text?" she said, angry despite herself.

"In the room of the departed," he said with a kind of chilly correctness. Lotte was frightened by this coldness and she said, "I must prepare myself." She knew the works of Rilke by heart. His poems were like the prayerbook with which she shut herself up in times of trouble. An evening devoted to Rilke, this was her life's dream, and like most of her dreams this one too had come to nothing.

The men carried the stretcher. At the head the janitor in his well-pressed blue suit, which gave him the air of a retired army officer, next to him Herbert wearing a gray jacket, like a high school teacher. Behind them Balaban, looking broad and strong.

They crossed the hillside at an angle. Faint, wintry shadows covered the slow, tortuous procession. From this vantage point the landscape was revealed in all its bare and leafless glory. Herbert turned his head, as if he was asking the company to approve the chosen site. They nodded their heads as a sign of approval.

The constraint was profound, and no one wept. They stood beside the open grave for a long time in silence. And but for the janitor who lifted his spade, they would have gone on standing there. The janitor filled in the hole and stuck the wooden sign into the loose earth. The sign, hastily carved only an hour before, was more expressive than anything else of Isadora's last request: discretion.

It was Lotte's turn. She was moved, and the words which she knew as intimately as a daily prayer emerged from her lips harsh and choked. All her experience on the stage seemed to drop away from her. The words scratched jarringly on the silent air. Lotte covered her face, as if she had failed shamefully.

After the funeral the cook opened the hatch and brought out hot coffee. Her face next to the hatch looked stiff and censorious. She did not utter a word as if she understood that this was not the time for words.

ELEVEN

With Isadora's death a new cold descended on the
retreat. No one spoke about it. They preferred to
speak of other matters, sad and remote, which had
preoccupied them all autumn long and now too did
not cease to trouble them. Lang rejoiced in his
achievements with a kind of boyish wonder which
made it impossible to be angry with him. Every
morning he ran all the way down to the village,
drank a tankard of beer and ate a country sandwich,
thereby killing two, or rather three, birds with one
stone. He exerted his muscles to make his body
strong, tasted healthy food and learned the local
dialect, bracing as beer to his palate.

Lang had been born in Galicia. He remembered
his native town well, but he did not like talking

about it. All his defects—his shortness, his long face, his broken accent—he blamed on the place of his birth, his corrupt inheritance. For this reason too he had never married, lived from hand to mouth and drifted from place to place. Two years ago he had decided to come up here to correct his defects, and he was doing so with praiseworthy perseverance.

Every morning he got up early, took a shower, put on his sports suit and ran down the hill. He spent most of the day down in the village, in the tavern and running along the riverbanks. And there was no denying it: he had changed. In his time Balaban had praised him and held him up as an example. When he came back in the evening he was not only too tired to take part in the arguments, gambling and card games, but he deliberately turned his back on them. The previous winter he had suffered from a chest complaint which had obliged him to retire to his room, but in the spring he had recovered his strength and ever since he had not missed even one morning run. Sometimes, in high spirits, he would stand and admire himself: his muscles. A kind of boyish wonder covered his face. It was hard to be angry with him.

When he heard of Isadora's sudden death he hid his face, wishing in this way to devote himself for a moment to the memory of the dead woman. Of all the people in the retreat, the one who had most enjoyed listening to him was Isadora. And although she had often mocked him, called him "shorty," "kurz," ridiculed him for his stupid running and described him as an incorrigible Jew, he liked her. On her sixty-fifth birthday he had made an enthusiastic speech about the new way of life, untainted by any speck of Jewishness, and called Isadora a naturally straightforward human being who detested all crookedness.

Lotte came back from the funeral in a dejected mood. Never before had she so disgraced herself. Not even as an inexperienced young trouper. Herbert sat next to her and comforted her as if she was in mourning. What are you talking about, your reading was great, powerful, incisive. His consolations sweetened her shame a little and she cried.

"I'm ashamed."

"You are a great actress." Herbert raised his voice as if she were deaf. Strange, this compliment, intended only to shut her up, had its effect. She stopped crying, like a child seduced by false promises. Balaban took the opportunity to confess. The dirty little town of his birth was still rooted in his heart. Perhaps because he had run away without leaving a note or writing a letter. If only he had said goodbye, the separation would have been final. But since he had not said goodbye, he remembered them all, one by one. Especially his sister Tzili. Her quiet, clever eyes. Although he spoke of himself and his secret pain, it seemed as if he were speaking to Isadora, appeasing her and begging her forgiveness.

That night nobody played cards or gambled. They sat and spoke of their memories, as if they wanted to meet Isadora in her new home, invisible to the naked eye.

For two years she had lived among them and how little they knew about her. Apart from her name, her surname, her birthday—nothing. Such pride and reserve; but her daughters, the daughters to whom Isadora had given the best musical education with the most famous teachers in Berlin and Rome, thought that their mother was a nuisance, a nag, irritatingly maternal and too Jewish for comfort. Accordingly, there was no more suitable place for her in the whole of Austria than Balaban's retreat. They had not even taken the trouble of bringing her up the mountain. A coachman had brought her there.

Isadora, who detested Jewish institutions and organizations from the bottom of her heart, who avoided everything Jewish like the plague, had been banished not by strangers but by her own daughters to the Jews and their shamefulness, exposed for every eye to see. But you had to hand it to Isadora: her hostility to her origins, up to the very end, was total and uncompromising. Even her daughters' treachery did not soften her attitude toward the Jews.

TWELVE

And while the winter winds blew cruelly over the bare mountain slopes Mrs. Kron packed her blue suitcase and announced that she was leaving. Strange, in the days preceding this decision her face had not expressed displeasure: on the contrary, she had had much to say in favor of the place. She was often to be seen in the company of Lang, discussing the beneficial effects of the mountain air. Lang, for his part, was full of optimism. His daily run in the frost filled his skinny body with the determination to overcome his weaknesses. She asked many detailed questions, and Lang kept nothing from her. Isadora's death was not forgotten, but it cast less gloom.

And suddenly, as if waking from a nightmare, she packed her bag and said, "I'm leaving."

"What have we done wrong?" said Lang in surprise, spreading both thin hands.

"I'm going home."

"In that case we can all go. If anyone can decide to leave in a moment of weakness, what will become of the rest of us?"

"She had not, apparently, expected to hear words like these. She bowed her head and said, in a womanly voice, "I left a home, didn't I?"

"What home are you talking about?"

"My home in the Herngasse."

"I don't understand," said Lang. "I need more information."

"Isn't it clear?"

"No, it isn't. Not to me at any rate."

Mrs. Kron put her case down and took off her gloves with a very domestic air. She said again, "Isn't it clear?"

Lang gathered his courage together and said, "We all have homes down below. But of our own free will and in full possession of our senses we decided that for the good of us all we must change our former way of life, eradicate our defects for once and for all."

"I?"

"All of us. Each to the extent of his own defects. And our defects are numerous, not so?"

"And wht about my home? I was very attached to my home."

"It will wait for you. No one will break into private property, and in the meantime you will absorb something of the healthful splendors of the winter. Winter up here, if I may say so, is magnificent."

And true enough, the morning light was clear and cold outside the windows. The universe at this moment seemed full of energy. The hatch opened and coffee was served in heavy mugs.

"Won't you have some coffee?"

"With pleasure," she said, as if she had forgotten her previous intention.

Lang hurried to the hatch and brought her a cup of coffee. The other inmates were apparently still asleep, shaving or shaking out blankets on the cold back porch. In the hall, at any rate, only a few people were to be seen, and they too seemed in no hurry to approach the hatch. The morning hour stood calm and still, as if time was not measured there by clocks.

"I didn't know you had a house in *Herngasse*."

"I left the keys with my sister. My sister, I must tell you, is married to a very wealthy and prominent man."

"I understand," said Lang. "I'm sure she must be looking after the house."

"I suppose so."

"In that case, why the rush?"

"An uneasy feeling," said Mrs. Kron, and shuddered a little at the sound of her own words.

"Such feelings must be overcome. These little worries can drive us out of our minds," said Lang in a stern but gentle tone.

"You're quite right."

"I've made up my mind, come what may, nothing is going to deflect me from my purpose any more."

"I'm sorry to say," said Mrs. Kron in a thin, somewhat choked voice, "that there are many things which worry me and disturb my peace of mind."

"That's not good," said Lang dryly.

"My elder sister Blanca is determined to make me convert. I have to admit that she is a very intelligent woman, very brave. She converted when she was still a girl."

"And what did you say to her," asked Lang carefully.

"I told her that I couldn't bring myself to do it."

"And what did she say?"

"She disagreed with me."

"And now you want to go down and convert."

Mrs. Kron giggled. It was a rather silly little giggle.

In the meantime a number of people had gathered outside the hatch. Trude dished out the coffee and peasant bread with a mean hand. The people took their portions and remained standing where they were. The dimly lit hall seemed frozen in immobility.

"I have no intention of converting." Mrs. Kron resumed her train of thought.

"There's no need of that. No need at all. The air here is good. The food healthy, the walks delightful."

"Very true."

"There are a lot of crude people down below. I can't stand crude people."

"You're quite right."

"I would give this simple way of life another chance. It promises much."

And thus he succeeded in appeasing her. She took her suitcase back to her room. Lang, pleased with his powers of persuasion, embarked upon a lengthy description of everything that had happened to him since his decision to come to the retreat. As he spoke his language grew increasingly bombastic. He spoke of a great nation whose way of life had been corrupted, and which now had no alternative but to rectify the many defects it had accumulated. Each of them separately and all of them together. The cheerful, modest happiness left his face and a boyish earnestness shone from his eyes. Mrs. Kron was drawn to his words as if by magic.

"But not everybody understands these things," he said sadly.

"New ideas don't catch on easily."

"That's true," said Lang, surprised by her response.

Now it was her turn to appease him. She wanted to cheer him up.

Lang sank for a moment into his thoughts. Mrs. Kron rose to the occasion. "There are good conditions for physical activity here," she said. "Fresh air, open spaces and a gymnastics hall. In the final analysis a man must take his fate in his own two hands."

"The time has come for my morning run. I must go now." Lang rose to his feet. For some reason he looked shorter than usual.

"Go, my dear," said Mrs. Kron in a motherly voice.

"It's very cold out. Five hundred meters will be enough today."

"Quite enough," she agreed.

THIRTEEN

The next day people played cards again with all the old passion. The cook emerged from the kitchen and stood on one side, watching their enthusiasm with wrathful vigilance, beside herself with anger. In the past, when she and Balaban had worked together as a team, she would burst in and hurl abuse at the card players, but ever since Balaban had defected and begun to play cards and gamble himself, she no longer appeared in the hall but shut herself up in the kitchen, seething with venom.

Among the inmates there were a few who really knew how to take life lightly and enjoy themselves, for instance, Lauffer. Like the others, he too had arrived here not entirely of his own free will, but he had immediately realized that the place had advantages of its own: chess in the mornings, coffee and cake at five o'clock, farm girls in the village. If there was anyone the cook hated, it was Lauffer. All the Jewish vices were personified in him. On her lips his name was a warning and a lesson. Not so the other residents, who had grown accustomed to his weaknesses, and enjoyed his jokes, the way he dressed, sold his watches and wasted his money.

At one time he had been married to a gentile woman, an educated woman of the middle classes who played the piano and read books. Lauffer had been captivated by her charms, but it soon transpired that he had made a mistake. She was an incorrigible Christian. For a year she refrained from going to church, but at the end of the year she reverted to her old ways. Lauffer, to tell the truth, did not attach much importance to her beliefs, referring to them in the language of his generation as "atavistic beliefs," but the smell of incense which she brought back with her from church drove him out of his mind. He tried to make jokes about it, in his usual way, but she was firm. And to make things worse she actually hung a picture of the Virgin Mary on the bedroom wall. Soon after that they separated. The marriage had lasted six years and he was forty when the separation took place. Since then he had drifted from place to place and from one occupation to another. He even had a haberdashary shop in Salzburg.

Now he was here, free of responsibility. He had a bit of cash, a few watches, a little foreign currency.

In short: a penny or two with which to gladden the heart of a woman. And since at Balaban's retreat the frivolous, the lazy, the idle and the short were hounded mercilessly, he was unwittingly transformed into a modest advocate of the Jewish way of life.

"I have never loved the Jews. Lovers of the Jews, if they exist at all, are few and far between, I think. But one thing must be said to their credit. They detest cabbage."

"Jewish food, you must admit, is difficult to digest."

"You should try it. It's not as bad as you think."

"I'm prepared to do without it."

"Not me."

"I'd sell you the lot for a mess of pottage."

"And I'd buy it."

"How much will you give?"

"What a question—all I have."

This argument with Lang had been going on for months. Sometimes in passing, and sometimes at length, but never with animosity, for it was not Lauffer's way to censure or condemn. "We're all of us only temporary lodgers here," he would say, "here today and gone tomorrw. As long as they give you a cup of coffee and let you smoke a cigarette, make the most of it." But it was precisely this nonchalance that drove certain people out of their minds. Especially the cook. She forgave him nothing. And when he appeared at the hatch she filled his bowl with contempt. These Jews make me sick, she said once through clenched teeth.

Lauffer looked like a traveling salesman, or a small-scale speculator. The kind you can meet in a café of a morning, without dignity or charm. The residents still remembered his arrival. He came with two little parcels and stood in the doorway. Balaban refused to admit him, on the grounds that he was an incorrigible Jew. To a certain extent he was right: Lauffer would not exercise or run. Give Lauffer a cup of coffee and a piece of cheesecake, a cigarette and a young woman—not too young—he could treat to a hearty meal in a good restaurant, and he would do himself proud, but running up and down a mountain: no, there was no power on earth that could make him do it. From this point of view, and not only this point of view, he was a true member of his race: frivolous, nimble, shifty as they come and capable of exerting a spellbinding charm on gentile women. When Balaban spoke to him a strange smile spread over his lips. And while Lang and his like ran and exercised, tried to stand up straight, swam and lifted weights, Lauffer had nothing in his head but thoughts of small indulgences and treats. But for his good nature he would have been hated even more. He was generous, of that there could be no doubt. From time to time he would bring back from the village honey cake, fish fried in butter, poppy-seed rolls or a jar of strawberry jam. On the late Isadora's birthday he had bought a bottle of expensive liqueur. Isadora had been unable to endure his company, calling him frivolous like all his race, but he, for some reason, did not hold it against her.

If there was anyone in the street who knew the value of a tasty dish, a fragrant perfume, a feminine bauble, it was Lauffer. At one time people would argue with him and blame him, and Balaban once declared in a rage, "If any of you would like to know the true figure of a Jew, look at Lauffer and you'll understand why people hate us. They're right to hate us." Since then a lot of water had passed beneath the bridge, and people had changed. Life at these heights, there was no denying, had its effect.

But not on the cook. She sat in the kitchen, seething with venom. If her anger had faded, her envy had not.

"What do the gentile women see in him, be so good as to explain. His height is no height. His clothes, no clothes. His appearance is the perfection of ugliness. What do the gentile women see in him that they are so drawn to him?"

"They aren't drawn to him. He draws them."

"What does he draw them with?"

"I don't know. With perfume, I suppose."

Mirzel sitting in the kitchen and listening knew: Lauffer was kind hearted. He understood women, he knew how to listen to them and how to whisper in their ears. No wonder they loved him.

FOURTEEN

The accursed memories. But for the memories life
on the mountain would have been different. People
would perhaps have found a measure of reconcilia-
tion. The long winter nights, they all agreed,
weren't easy. You were alone with yourself, with
no barriers. A number of them were driven mad by
their longings and they escaped, some to the son or
daughter who had denied them, some into the
anonymous arms of the cold.

Lotte was happy about her grant. Life was not
particularly glorious but it was no longer burden-
some. A dormant seed of optimism budded in her.
She slept a lot, or sat observing people. To tell the
truth, she spent many hours brooding about her
childhood home. Her father, whose modest passion

for books had caused family quarrels. Now too the thought that she had inherited a number of his physical defects did not endear him to her.

"Thank you," she had said to Herbert.

"Why thank me?" said Herbert. "The board had objective criteria for its choice."

For hours she sat musing about the past. And when the fog became too thick to penetrate she began to brood again about her body and its lack of proportion, her spectacles, wrinkles and blemishes.

Herbert said, "I offered up my life to Moloch."

"What Moloch are you referring to?"

"Like all Jews, the journalistic Moloch."

"Strange, everyone has his own Moloch."

"What do you mean? You were in the theater."

"If second-rate one-acters and erotic jokes constitute the art of the theater, then I was a faithful disciple of the art."

People didn't always talk. For the most part they asked questions. One of them would take his question and pose it in the air of the hall, without expecting a reply. But someone passing there by chance would hear his question and answer it. The answer was seldom given in full. And sometimes there was a mumble of agreement or protest, or a sudden flash of memory, which was a kind of answer in itself. It sometimes happened too that conversations were detailed and lengthy, going on, with interruptions, for many hours. This was what happened to Lotte. Herbert went down with the

102

janitor to bring potatoes. She was standing by the window and gazing at the snow. For some reason the word "Moloch" stuck in her head and conjured up the vision of a kind of circus freak. And while she was standing absorbed in her vision and horrified by its yellow colors one of the inmates approached her and introduced himself: Bruno Rauch. One of the senior residents. He still remembered the retreat in the good old days, the bracing, disciplined days when they got up early and went to bed early, ate peasant bread and yogurt for breakfast and worked on their accents.

"Do you miss those days?" asked Lotte.

"Of course. They were great days, days of the reform of body and soul. But how could I possibly forget them."

"But they weren't easy, I think."

"Indeed they weren't. But they were days with a purpose. Once a man realizes that his body is weak and ugly, his nerves destroyed, his soul corrupt, that he bears within him a decayed inheritance, in short, that he is sick and, what is worse, that he is passing his sickness on to his children, what can he desire more deeply than reform?"

"Interesting," said Lotte.

"No doubt about it, the beginning was magnificent. And the continuation too was not lacking in success. I myself, if I may be permitted to introduce a personal note, felt a far-reaching change."

"In what sphere, may I ask?"

"My nerves, in the first place, grew calmer. All the members of our race suffer from weak nerves, and it is via these unsound, inflamed organs that they gain their impressions of the world. You must admit, madam, that an idea of the world which comes from inflamed nerves is not the most reliable. Panic and haste, madam, are the authors of all our sins. And I suddenly felt that I was growing calmer, and the others felt the same. What more could anyone desire?"

"Wonderful," Lotte, for some reason, replied.

"And our height too, madam. I wouldn't go so far as to say that we actually grew taller, but our posture changed. A straight back, madam, is an indication of change. Certainly of a change in one's perception of the world. The Jews, we cannot deny, suffer from many defects. I myself have counted two hundred defects—no small number in relation to one human being."

"And others have no defects."

"Others too, of course. But their defects are healthy. People say that the Austrians are heavy drinkers. Of course they are, but that, if it can be called a defect at all, is a healthy defect. A man forgets himself for an hour, which is healthy for him and everyone else. If only the Jews knew how to drink, to relax, they would surely be different—stronger, braver, perhaps even more honest. But the Jews are rodents: not for nothing does the world regard them as animals of the rodent species. I myself, madam, what was I all those years, but a rodent? Balaban, in the simplicity of his heart, understood it better than we did."

"I was told that in the beginning he was very harsh."

"Correct, he was harsh. And isn't the doctor harsh when he forces his patient to take bitter medicines, injects him or amputates infected limbs? Of course there is a certain degree of harshness here, but deep-seated diseases are not eradicated by aspirin."

"And you still remember him at the height of his powers."

"Yes, of course. He was completely different. He looked like a farmer, fantastically healthy. The kind of health which is conceivable only in people who work the land. He wanted to share his health with us. And so he did, with the most praiseworthy success. We, the first inmates, will never forget it. His defection is something I shall never understand. We must have infected him with our own frivolity. A great shame." He spoke quietly, in a balanced, unemotional tone, as if he was talking about some investment which had not made a good profit. And, in fact, he was a banker by profession. This profession had left its traces in his hands, his gestures, his expression and his eyes with their look of suffering and reserve.

"And you, madam, have you accustomed yourself already to our way of life here?" he asked, with his old politeness.

"To a large extent."

105

"Do you exercise? You are an actress, I believe."

"That is correct."

In that case it must be easier for you. Actors are used to physical training. For us the first year was particularly difficult. I must tell you, madam, that I was a sedentary creature all my life and my only contact with the land took place in the summer vacations."

"And you gave up your position?"

"Of my own free will and in full possession of my senses. A man must face his defects in the end. My wife, I must tell you, is not of our race."

"She comes to visit you from time to time, I suppose."

"No. I forbade her to visit me. In a place like this a man must be by himself."

"When do you think of going back?"

"Not for some time to come."

He looked about fifty-five years old. He was not a tall man. There was a quiet kind of seriousness in his voice, as if he was speaking of some religious experience for which he was preparing himself.

FIFTEEN

In February Balaban succumbed to dark, angry moods. From time to time he would burst into the hall and lash out with barely intelligible grunts and growls. "None of you are ready," he growled. "What will you do if the horse trainers come? What did I bring you here for? You're eating up all my property." Cries and shouts which had once been the terror of stable and barn. But in spite of his threats the inmates were not really frightened. And Balaban, apparently sensing that his anger was not making an impression, would smash a plate or throw a pot to the floor.

Herbert would stand next to him and calm him down, speak to him in mild and conciliatory words, humor him and promise him that in the summer everything would be better, the inmates would come to their senses, run like deer and exercise. From time to time Balaban would go down to the village, get drunk and come back red in the face, exuding a sour smell and muttering in the language of a stable boy. The Jews were loafers, cheats, liars, money-grubbers and gamblers. There was no hope for them but a forced labor camp.

Betty Shlang's gaiety did not abandon her even in these hard times. She would make her appearance in the hall, nonchalantly scattering compliments. The inmates treated her tolerantly, as if she were a troublesome sister who was not quite right in the head. Toward Balaban, for some reason, she was particularly provocative.

"So you intend changing me."

"Yes, you too."

"You hear, he wants to change me. How do you want to change me?"

"By exercise, of course, running every morning and working the land."

"Me."

"Yes, you. It's about time."

Two years before she had divorced her husband and ever since she had been celebrating her freedom. She changed her dress twice a day, made up her face and kept up an endless stream of old Jewish jokes, giving the place the air of a pension in bygone days: small talk and flirtations.

She had arrived here by mistake, under the impression that it was a cheap hotel of the kind commonly encountered in the provinces. But as time went by, although she never actually realized her mistake, she adjusted herself to the life of the retreat and turned into a permanent fixture, one of the loyal old-timers without whom the place would have been unthinkable. Like the others, she too was planning to return to the plains in a month or two. They had grown accustomed to her chatter, and no one told her to keep quiet any more.

She had wanted to go on the stage when she was a girl, but her parents had been horrified at the idea and prevented her from fulfilling her ambition. Later on she married. The marriage was childless, but nevertheless her husband too had prevented her from becoming an actress. For this she would never forgive him. And in order to show off her theatrical gifts she would recite, sing like a barmaid, and take off the rabbi in the temple. Her performances were rather lacking in taste or talent, but they were amusing nevertheless. But for her mortal enemy the cook, her life would have been easier. The cook hounded her and called her emptyheaded Betty, and whenever she had the opportunity to deprive her of breakfast or supper she was only to glad to do so. Betty for her part mimicked her, told jokes about her, and when she was feeling particularly sour she called her a holy harlot.

In the course of time it became clear that she was bent on attracting the notice of Robert, the janitor.

In the beginning Balaban had brought Robert from the village in order to teach the inmates how to work in the fields, ride horses and swim in the river. He was a tall, laconic man. People still remembered how he had guided them on long walks, taken care of the horses and worked in the garden. He did his work quietly and impassively, and when the sun set he would drop onto his bed and fall asleep. But after a year on the mountain something changed in him. At first the change seemed insignificant, but as time went by it transpired that he was taking an increasing interest in the idle chatter and poker games of the inmates. Balaban reprimanded him, but he kept his eyes open and learned in secret. Balaban meant to fire him, but he lacked the resolution to do so.

From time to time he would go down to the village and get drunk and come back happy. But it was no longer the same happiness. He took to sitting on the ground with a gloomy expression on his face, and he would often fall asleep where he sat.

"What is to become of you, Robert?" Balaban would say to him from time to time.

"What?"

"I'm asking you what is to become of you. I brought you here in order to reform these Jews. To get them out-of-doors, straighten their backs, make honest men of them."

At first he would make excuses, tell stories and lies. But now when he saw Balaban coming he would slink away like a guilty animal. Sometimes when the fancy took him he would talk about his village, life in the country, his crops and his animals. He had a soft spot in particular for deciduous fruit trees: plums and peaches. And when he sat and spoke about these things his old expression would come back to him. And thus, without intending it, he kindled longings in people's hearts and awoke dormant desires to go down to the plains. Betty was enchanted by his voice, but he disapproved of Betty and her eccentricities.

It was no longer a secret to anyone that at night she cried aloud: Robert, I love you, your body born from the trees of the fields, your eyes washed by the rivers, your soul hewn from the source of purity. And sometimes, beside herself, she would ask shamelessly: "Why doesn't he want to go to bed with me? Isn't my body good enough to go to bed with any more?"

"You must exercise. He's not used to Jewish women."

"I'm a woman and that's all. What's Jewish about me, for God's sake?"

"You must speak to him quietly."

"How can I be calm? He's driving me out of my mind."

At one time, it was no secret, he had conducted a number of modest flirtations with the women residents, some said with Sophia too. But since Sophia's death he had been sunk in a stupor and

111

hardly uttered a word. If not for Betty, his presence would scarcely have attracted any attention at all. But precisely his comatose state, his quiet, bucolic drowsiness, drove her wild. He sleeps with himself, she muttered, why not with me? What am I asking for, after all. Nothing but a little caress. The cook listened and ground her teeth. If it had been in her power to throw Betty out, she would have thrown her out. But to her credit it must be said that Betty sometimes forgot herself and her tormenting desires, her grudges and grievances against her ex-husband, put on a dress with an impressively low neckline, and sat in the hall telling old Jewish jokes. And although everybody knew these jokes by heart, no one told her to keep quiet.

Lang, however, persevered. Even when the temperature dropped to below zero he went on exercising. Sometimes he managed to drag Rauch with him, and they ran round the mountain together. And when Betty saw them running in the frost she jumped up like a startled girl and cried, "Look at them running. Who told them to run like that?"

The end of February was fresh, clear and transparent as glass. From the front windows the slopes looked blindingly smooth and clear. What am I doing here, a voice rose distractedly in the air. What do you mean, have you forgotten? You're here to reform your character, correct your defects, straighten your distortions. And the crooked shall be made straight, isn't that what it says in the Bible?

The old Jewish mockery blossomed round the tables, where the card games now continued from morning to night. From time to time Lauffer brought a bottle of brandy up from the village and they all drank a toast. And if there was anyone who was persecuted for nothing, it was the janitor. Balaban could not forgive him his sins, and whenever Balaban appeared in the hall he slunk away. The horse too was no longer what it had been. It could barely manage to draw the old sleigh. Every now and then the janitor went out to the stable and beat it up, more than anything else in order to create a little commotion so that Balaban would not suspect him of sitting about doing nothing.

But Lotte was happy. The idea that she had been awarded a grant never ceased to gladden her heart. At first she thought of preparing Ibsen's Nora, but then she changed her mind. Now she was working on Rilke. She still had not found the right tone. Poetry reading was a complex art, as she knew to her cost. She saw Herbert only rarely. He was working. Once a day he went down with the janitor to buy provisions. On his return he looked like a tired Jewish businessman. He grew tanned, and there was a kind of wondering bewilderment on his face.

Lotte's days now passed in a strange, vivid clarity. The inward clamor, did not subside. But it was no longer a devouring clamor, it was a steady flow of water gathering to a point. She liked observing people closely: their hands and feet, the way they sat, rested, ate. A head suddenly tilting to the left. It was a soundless hunt which absorbed her for hours, so intensely that it hurt. When her heart was stirred, she would put on her coat and go out to walk around the building, the remains of the stables and the running field, Balaban's kingdom sinking beneath the snow. And when she returned from her walk, she would wrap herself in the thin blankets and sit in the hall. It was very cold, and the heating was not working. If only Balaban had installed an old-fashioned stove they would have been able to chop up wood and heat the hall. But the coal for the heating system had to be brought up from the village and it was expensive. At the beginning of winter Balaban would appear and announce: "Cold strengthens the body. Take an example from Lang." Now he no longer said anything, and besides, he was hardly ever to be seen in the hall.

As Lotte sat shivering under the two thin blankets a man approached her and offered her a sheepskin, saying, "This will keep you warm."

"But I can't take it, it's yours," said Lotte.

"I have another one. I provided myself with whatever I needed. I didn't rely on anybody."

"And you're giving this one to me?"

"I have an extra one. I bought it in the village last summer. I told them all: prepare yourselves. Winter's coming. And Balaban won't do anything about the heating. But they wouldn't listen, I'm sorry to say, and now they're freezing."

114

"You were right."

"I told them not to give him money. I knew he wouldn't do anything about the heating, but they shut their ears and gave him all they had. And now they're freezing."

"You were quite right," said Lotte, sensing that the man was in need of a word of approval.

"What good are words when people refuse to listen."

The practicality of this man, who looked about fifty, horrified her. She looked at his little, waxen hands, which for some reason made her think of the Jewish peddlers she had encountered on her travels, bowed down under the weight of their cases. Sometimes they would push their way into the rehearsal hall and offer their wares for sale.

"And another thing," the man continued without waiting for a reply, as if he was afraid something would prevent him from passing on this important information, "don't trust anybody and don't expect any favors," he whispered.

"I don't expect anything," said Lotte.

"In that case you're on the right path, the only right one. Illusion is the mother of all sin, and here, I'm sorry to say, everyone is party to the illusion."

"Thank you very much," said Lotte.

"Not at all. When all's said and done, I can't do much to help you. There's only one thing I wanted to say: don't expect any favors." He repeated this slogan and it seemed as if he had learned it off by

115

heart. His pale face, blotched with orange freckles, lost its serious expression, softened and he smiled.

"People here still write letters and ask for favors from the ones they left below. God almighty, what self-deception."

"And you yourself have no relations below?"

"Of course I have, two sons. But I had them converted when they were still young, while I still had a little control over them. I would never have dared to do it when my wife was alive. My wife was a proud Jewess, from the East. But I knew I had no right to imprison them in the cage called a Jewish ghetto and I gave them the freedom to choose—an observation point. So that they wouldn't come and blame their father for bequeathing them a malignant disease. Their father did what had to be done. Now let them carry on."

"Do they write?"

"No. I told them explicitly not to write to me. It's too late now for me to change and I don't want to change. I'm satisfied with my lot. By the way, I never believed in Balaban's experiments, begging his pardon. I don't fancy the taste of his miracle yogurt, I detest hunting, hate sport, nobody's going to change me at this stage of my life, not even with a whip. But my sons—with my sons it's another story. I had them converted when they were still boys at high school. They married young and they live in the country. Good luck to them. It's good for them to be there in the fresh air close to the farm animals. What did I have to give to them: only shame, feelings of fear. I haven't seen them for ten years now. I'm sure that I wouldn't recognize them if I saw them. They probably speak the local dialect by now. Tell me, don't you think I did right?"

And Lotte, suddenly forced to respond, did not know what to say. Cold shivers ran down her spine. She bent down and tried to hide her face.

"My considerations were very practical: good and evil, life and death. I chose good, I chose life. Should I perhaps have spoiled my sons' lives for the sake of a few paternal sentiments? The dead are forgotten in the end. And what I spoiled nature will put right, the women and the animals of the fields."

"And don't you miss them?"

"No, to tell the truth. I'm a practical man, madam. I feel comfortable with my own kind. I know them and they know me. And here, at any rate, it's every man for himself. He who has a blanket is warm and he who lacks one suffers from the cold. We were born Jews and it seems we shall die Jews. Let's not leave any traces beyond what's strictly necessary." His businesslike tone seemed to falter and he dropped his voice to a whisper. "Balaban tried to tame me too, he took me out to run in the morning a couple of times. What a joke. And when I laughed he called me an incorrigible Jew. What does he want me to do, cry?"

"Supper." The cook opened the hatch and rang a little bell. The man's face emerged with a start from his stream of words and he hurried off to fetch his bowl. "Au revoir," he said. "My name is Max Hammer. We'll meet again."

The sharp, sudden sound split Lotte's attention in two like a ball cut in half. She now knew, with a new clarity, that her achievements in the theater were small and insignificant, that her characterizations were weak, and that she had never plumbed the depths of a single role.

Everyone was standing in the queue and she too joined them. The way they were standing there, so still, reminded her of some forgotten theatrical piece. She now felt a sad kind of intimacy with these people, who had come to shelter under the wings of Balaban.

That night Lotte wrapped herself in the sheepskin and she did not feel the cold at all. The figure of the short man did not leave her for a moment. His practical matter-of-factness for some reason filled her with pity. To tell the truth she felt pity for herself, for her life which had passed in haste and confusion.

SIXTEEN

And while the cold spread over the bare slopes,
locking the retreat within its strong arms, Lang disappeared. At first it seemed nothing but a trifling
lateness. For he did sometimes come late. But when
evening fell and Lang had still not come back, a few
people gathered in the doorway.

Recently he had been full of enthusiasm, speaking of his own transformation and the transformation of the others with many bombastic
words. In the retreat they still remembered his dramatic cry, full of pathos: There is still hope! A few
of them had in fact noticed that something had
changed in his appearance, but who paid any attention to such trivialities? Everyone was preoccupied

with his own concerns: blankets and something hot to drink. Balaban made desperate attempts but lighting a fire in the stove was beyond him.

The anxiety spread of its own accord. They spoke of other days, different conditions, of the gymnastic apparatus lying uselessly in the deserted gym hall, of Betty Shlang and all her fantasies which had now been subsumed in one compelling vision: Robert.

And while they were all talking, arguing and complaining, Balaban rose to his feet, put on his farmer's coat and announced in his old voice: "We must go out to look for him." The announcement was short and clipped, every word showed resolution. And he did not stop at words. He divided the residents into teams, appointed a leader for every team, distributed a torch, a rope and a hunting knife to each, and with no more ado commanded: "Every man to his post. No one will be abandoned."

The residents were thunderstruck. It was a long time since words of this caliber had been heard in the retreat. True, in the days of his glory Balaban had shown a certain firmness and resolution. But many months had passed since then. The old habits had come creeping back and found a refuge here.

"I told him," said Mrs. Kron in her old maternal voice, "but he wouldn't listen to me. He refused to give up his evening run. What sane person goes running in the winter, in the frost?" Rauch, his morning running mate, stood wrapped up in his winter coat, silent and erect, looking for some reason like the possessor of vast properties. To tell the truth, it was Betty who was now the center of attention. She ranted and raved, screaming at the top of her voice. "What am I doing here? Why did I let myself be talked into staying here?" Her outburst was a mixture of words, complaints and ancient fears. Herbert's pleas were in vain. She was insistent: What am I doing here.

"Becoming a human being," said Rauch, raising his voice.

"I'm a woman."

"You're a jellyfish, not a woman."

"Did you hear what he called me?" Betty interrupted her screaming.

This exchange, for some reason, relieved the tension.

Order, needless to say, was not maintained. The search party descended the hill, holding onto each other and shouting at the tops of their voices: "Lang, Lang, where are you? Give us a sign of life." And a certain satisfaction was felt. Some of them were reminded of scouting camps in the winter season, and some of the First World War. Then too people had gone out on search parties and lost their way.

After an hour of wandering about, talking and stumbling, Betty calmed down and caught up with the others. The snow fell thickly and covered the ground with a white blanket. The village houses stood wrapped in darkness. Balaban strode ahead without urging them on, and Rauch in his smart winter coat spoke, no longer with pathos but with absolute clarity, of the great obligation to go out into the snow and search for the lost and the brave. Questions of death and honor had engaged his mind in recent months. Of Lang he said that he had prepared himself for this hour. Life was precious, but not at any price.

Lotte now understood that she still had a long way to go in the art of public reading. Reading was like music, you had to make every note ring true, get the rhythm and the melody right. Perhaps she would have to begin again from the beginning. And then there were the veterans, the loyal fighters against weak bodies, broken accents, ugly Jewish gestures. These, for some reason, now celebrated the search with a few words not lacking in significance. A man is not an insect. The time for action has come at last.

And thus they advanced. Lang's disappearance seemed to have been forgotten. Their feet carried them forward, their sense of duty seemed to have found its proper course at last. And they were all pleased with themselves. Even Betty Shlang was pleased with herself for having succeeded in climbing down the mountain without slipping. She spoke at length about the queer legs which she had inherited from her parents. Her words sounded silly in the extreme, but since she walked without complaining nobody told her to keep quiet.

At midnight they found Lang near the tavern, drunk as a lord. The local brew, it appeared, had proved too strong for him. He sat on the ground with his legs crossed and delivered a long and confused monologue about himself, his past and the future of the Jewish people. Balaban was in a good mood and called him "My friend." "My friend, why sit on the ground," he said.

"It's not cold. The snow is my comrade and my bosom friend," said Lang poetically.

"True, very true," said Balaban, speaking slowly in a mild, calm voice. "But, nevertheless, don't you want to come home?"

"I am at home. Nature is my home. There's no home to beat it. So peaceful."

"But wouldn't you like to have a cup of coffee with us?"

"I have no need of such things any more," said Lang, pulling up the sleeve of his peasant shirt and exposing his arm, a thin, delicate arm. He rubbed it with snow and displayed it to them. "This arm no longer knows the meaning of fear."

The dialogue went on for a long time. And Lang was not satisfied until he had taken off his shirt and announced: "This snow no longer has any effect on me at all. Jewish fear is behind me."

Balaban did not scold or shout. He spoke to him quietly and cunningly, as if he were a disobedient animal, coaxing him to put on his shirt and rise to his feet. Strong men, he said, always stand on their

123

own two feet. And wonder of wonders, it worked. Lang stood up and said, "If it's a question of walking, I know how to walk." And he walked. And as he walked he spoke again of the Jewish fears which were the source of all their defects and weaknesses. They had to be pulled up by the roots. Balaban was pleased with these remarks and asked him questions.

In the early hours of the morning the weary convoy returned. Lang dropped to the floor and fell asleep. The snow was still falling, covering the windows with a thick layer of white. They were all pleased with themselves. They drank coffee and made jokes. Balaban sat down, an expression of great satisfaction on his broad face. He spoke about his early days in the famous Krautkraft stables. It was there, to tell the truth, that he had learned his trade. And although he used the language of stable boys and grooms there was no coarseness in his voice. It was as if he were seeing them from a great distance.

Lang lay curled up on the floor, his face dirty and confused. It was hard to tell if he was still drunk. His mouth was open and he breathed rhythmically. No one approached him. But for Mrs. Kron, who hurried off to fetch a blanket to cover him, his presence on the floor would have been forgotten.

SEVENTEEN

But not every day brought grace and salvation. The financial situation of the retreat went from bad to worse, a state of affairs which could no longer be hidden. Herbert went to the provincial capital once a week to sell Isadora's jewelry. And when he returned the expression on his face was not encouraging. He looked bowed and downcast. The price of coal had gone up. Potatoes too were not cheap. Balaban no longer spoke of important, spiritual matters but of his rapidly dwindling resources. If only they had worked in the garden in summer there would now be potatoes and cabbages in the cellar. There would be something to cook. It was true, not everyone had worked, but some had. They had tried their best, but the sowing had not been a success. Robert thought that the birds were to blame, the wicked birds had ruined the crop. At the time Balaban had been well content, even developed a special vocabulary to express his satisfaction. But all this, of course, was forgotten in the new circumstances and the cold winter.

And while winter raged at the door, the old standard-bearers came to life again, as if rising up from the dead. We didn't come here to eat and sleep and play cards and listen to the empty-headed chatter of Betty Schlang. We came here to uproot an old disease, corrupt characters, sick legs, to purify our souls. This was the voice of one of the old lecturers whom Balaban had brought to the mountain to lecture on Jewish abnormality. In recent months he had gone into a deep decline and secluded himself in his room. Now the old drive to preach and chastise reasserted itself.

He looked like a high school teacher, thin and sour-faced because of his old disease, the cursed ulcer which had troubled him since his youth. His voice had a special quality, stirring a man's soul until he knew that he was indeed weak, full of defects, lacking in will power and depressed to the point of despair. What was to be done about this melancholy, the enemy of humanity, which the Jews had fostered more than anyone else.

Ralph Glanz was a past master of this mood, intimate with all its secrets. There were times, not so far in the past, when he had held them all spellbound. The magic had dimmed, but not vanished. Especially when he spoke of the melancholy deeply embedded in the soul of our tribe. For the most part, he spoke of this subject in a whisper, with a kind of reverence for the subtle and unpredictable human sensation in question. A sad tribe which bequeathed its sadness to its children. But when he was in a bad mood he spoke of the same sensation in harsh, insulting words.

From his boyhood he had been afflicted by melancholy moods. And it was this melancholy which had ruined his life and spoiled his chances of advancement, a career, stability and a permanent post. The two articles he had published had been well received in the right quarters, but he had not persevered, he had let things slide, failed to follow up the necessary connections, left letters unanswered. All this and more had closed the doors of reputable academic institutions to him.

For over two years now he had been living on the mountain, subsidized by Herbert's grants. The trouble was that here too he did not write. He read, and he had a card file, but he had not been able to write. Herbert did not badger him. Far from it. Articles worthy of the name did not write themselves, there was plenty of time, the fund for art and research was a standing fund. The board chose the recipients of its grants with the greatest of care. But what was the use of all these consolations: he was not satisfied with himself.

Lotte's modest joy too was spoiled. A week before Engel had received a long, detailed letter from her ex-husband, Manfred. He was living in a little town called Shimitz, teaching singing in the local school. He had a number of private pupils, had organized a small band, and traveled to Warsaw once a week to buy books and sheet music. It was a small, traditional Jewish town. On Saturdays he too took part in the prayers. The place was remote, but the scenery was stunning, the people pleasant and hospitable. His income was small but he had security and enough to live on.

Lotte read the letter with astonishment. The voice was Manfred's voice, and in writing it seemed somehow even milder. Her life, which in the past few months had come to rest in this place, grew clamorous again. What am I doing here? Nobody wants me. As always, this time too she felt nothing but self-pity.

Sometimes she sat and spoke to Robert. "We were born flawed, we have to stay here. But you, a man of the land—what are you doing here?" she teased him.

"It's comfortable here."

"What comfort do you find here?"

"Sitting and talking."

"And in the village don't people talk?"

"Not at length."

"And don't you miss the fields?"

"I've been working for Jews for years."

"I never knew that. And how do you like them?"

"I've grown accustomed to them."

He was telling the truth. In his youth he had worked in a Jewish department store, then he had run away and tried country life again. But not long afterward he had returned to the city. He was strong and handsome, many women fell into his net. He had always worked, with occasional interruptions, for Jews. In their shops and their gardens. He did not like them, but he had grown used to their ways. They were easier to satisfy than the farmers and estate owners, it was easier to talk to them. They had good-looking women, and the women were generous with their favors. What more could a man ask for? A man should be content with his lot. There was truth in his quiet voice. As if he wasn't talking about his own fate, but about a law of nature. Now he was sixty-five years old, an age when a person should rest and not trouble his mind with strange ideas. If there was anything he missed, it was the mountains of his native village. But the village was far away and it was better not to think of it.

"And you have no complaints."

"No." As he said this he seemed to recover his peasant's face, and to Lotte he looked strong and ageless.

EIGHTEEN

But in the meantime Balaban fell ill. At first it seemed no more than a trifling cold, but when his fever did not drop Herbert decided to call the village doctor. The doctor, a converted Jew, refused to come at first, but in the end he came.

Balaban's illness was as strong as his body. With one blow it destroyed the language he had acquired at school, German, and gave him back his mother tongue. Now he spoke this tongue for hours on end. He recalled his parents and his brothers and sisters, calling them by many names, some of them incomprehensible. He blamed himself and accepted his punishment and fate.

Herbert sat by his bedside for hours and tried to calm him. "Your parents have forgiven you, believe me. They know that you never denied them in your heart. You always loved them. You'll still go back to them one day. That's the reason you came here in the first place, to help them." But Balaban refused to be consoled. He had not sent them money. What were they doing in this freezing cold?

"You did great things for the sake of the many," Herbert rebuked him.

"But I didn't take care of my sisters."

There were days too when he succumbed to foul, black moods, burned with fever and shouted to high heaven: all his property, the labor of years, had gone to the dogs. Strange, it was precisely these black moods which roused the inmates from their apathy. They exercised, ran, cleaned up and worked on their accents. Betty sat by the mirror for hours improving her accent. For years she had been trying to improve her acccent; her accent was to blame for the fact that she had not been accepted in the drama classes at the night school. Now she had the chance to improve. There were people here who knew what it meant to speak with a proper accent. The abandoned gym too came back to life. Even Lauffer, that shirker, exercised. Balaban's illness inspired people with a new spirit, they wanted to conciliate him. But Balaban was not satisfied: too late, he complained. There was a nasty sound to this combination of words, which he repeated whenever Herbert came to tell him that the inmates were exercising, cleaning the yard and improving their accents.

Late at night they read excerpts from Sophia's diary. During her short stay among them she had managed to fill a number of notebooks. She was forty-three years old when she died. She arrived on the mountain almost by accident. Herbert met her down below, in a café, and when he found out that she wrote poetry he invited her to join the retreat and offered her a grant. And Sophia, who was then at a crossroads in her life, saw this offer as a temporary solution and accepted.

Her life in the retreat was modest and secluded. She fought her battles in the privacy of her room, with her notebooks. She had a big coat in which she liked wrapping herself in the summer too. And it was thus that she would remain in their memories, wrapped up in her coat. It appeared that she had written very little about herself. She had observed the inmates closely in her search for vertical and horizontal lines, concave and convex shapes, everything that constituted form. Of Herbert she wrote: he reminds me of marble pillars veined with green. Polished, but still bearing within themselves the smell of the hills from which they had been quarried. Of the dead Isadora she had written: she courts death with broad, sweeping glances. As if to trap his fleeting steps. A noble beast of prey. Her opinion of Balaban was different: evil spirits were attacking him on every side. He tried to ignore them. But they were legion, malign, and they would overcome this lofty tree in the end.

In other passages she seemed to lose her steady, resolute vision. She spoke of her own weaknesses, of the fact that she had no roots in the soil, not this soil anyway, her writing lacked the sap of life. Sensitivity, even hypersensitivity, was not enough on which to found a life. The wood, the fibers, were the marrow. Without them all was fog and mist. And there was a special section too devoted to grace and honor. To the Jewish religion which was collective and tribal, and necessarily a religion of the herd. It trampled the honor of the individual underfoot. Christianity, in spite of everything, cherished the individual and believed in his salvation. It was clear that she had waged her battle with grim determination. And in her own words, the demons had won because they were stronger than human flesh and blood.

Balaban's illness dragged on. He refused to go to hospital. Every afternoon Herbert took him into the lobby. His face had changed beyond recognition, his cheeks were covered with stubble. He looked like a simple Jewish laborer. The language he had acquired so laboriously had been lost. He mumbled in a tongue which nobody understood. It was this metamorphosis, more than anything, which cast a gloom over the hall.

Herbert gradually lost even the modest egoism he had brought with him to the retreat. He no longer brooded about the journalistic hack work which had destroyed him, the dead wife he had loved, the

133

daughters who had denied him. He had no time for himself, he was busy working. Ever since Balaban's illness he had been managing the retreat and, to a certain extent, Balaban's collapsing business affairs too. Thieves, among them Jewish merchants, were devouring everything he possessed. Herbert tried to save what he could. Once a week he went down to the village, and sometimes twice, and when he returned he was pale with anger. But he recovered himself immediately, smiled good-naturedly, apologized for the poor food, the heating which did not work. He too had changed. His face was haggard and his fine gray curls had turned quite white. But his bearing still maintained a certain mute dignity.

Balaban's grumbling was hard to bear. When Herbert brought him out people scattered in all directions. Strange, it was this fear which brought the smell of the old days back to the retreat. If anyone was content, it was the cook. Her hard, austere face seemed to have found a temporary relief. The meager meals were served on time.

Balaban had brought Trude from Vienna. As a student she had been attracted to Christianity but her father, a simple Jew with opinions of his own, had asked her on his deathbed not to abandon the religion of her fathers, and she had promised him. She was true to her promise, but it wasn't easy. At first she went to work in a factory. At the end of the year she was elected to the workers' committee, and she waged a determined struggle with the owners to

134

improve conditions. This struggle earned her much respect, but as soon as her fellow workers discovered that she was a Jewess they dismissed her from the committee without a moment's hesitation. Not long afterward she was fired from her job. In the factory she had learned to get up early in the morning, persevere, and overcome the pain in her back. She never had a bad word to say about her life as a factory worker.

After that she went to work as an unregistered nurse at a hospital, in the sanitary department of the municipality. People who had known her father wanted to help her but she refused. She met Balaban in Vienna and was impressed by his personality. From her girlhood she had disliked the Jews. She thought that they were selfish and dishonest. She had not hidden these opinions from her father and she did not hide them from Balaban. Balaban thought she would be suitable for the post nevertheless and appointed her head cook of the retreat.

At the retreat people detested her. Even Robert, who avoided name-calling as a rule, called her the nun. She fought her battles grimly and harshly, and she was especially harsh to Mirzel, who broke the rules and served coffee and sandwiches outside regular hours. Trude made no overtures to the inmates and they made none to her. But she took it upon herself to keep the building scrupulously clean, and late at night, when everything was quiet, she would go from passage to passage cleaning and

135

polishing. Lately she had been working harder than ever. One night Lotte came across her in the passage and asked in surprise: "Are you still up?" Trude, kneeling on the floor, raised her eyes and said nothing. If Trude had dropped her eyes and gone back to work Lotte would have walked past, but Trude stared at her with a baffled look in her eyes.

"Do you need help?" asked Lotte.

"No," she said, and a tight little smile appeared at the corners of her lips.

"I'll help you with pleasure. I can't fall asleep."

"I'm used to it. I've worked all my life," said Trude simply.

"Where did you work?"

"In a factory, the second shift. Ever since then I find it difficult to sleep at night."

"And have you no relatives down below?"

"No."

"I have a daughter. Her name is Julia. I haven't seen her for ages. She finds it difficult to get up here, it seems."

"You're an actress, aren't you?"

"I worked in the theater for many years. Small parts, on the whole. Something inside me, perhaps my appearance too, prevented me from getting to the top."

"I'm sorry," said Trude. It was evident that she had not conversed with anyone for many months. The words came out loudly.

"No, I'm making an effort to improve. I'm preparing a selection of Rilke's poems. The grant has made it possible for me to prepare myself."

"I'm glad," said Trude.

"I'm trying my best. I don't know if I'll succeed."

"It must be hard work."

"I work on every sentence. Nothing less will do, it seems to me."

Trude laughed softly. As if a breeze had brushed her cheek. Lotte continued: "Because of my appearance I was always given servants' parts to play. Later on I grew tired of trying."

"You must try. We must always try," said Trude. Her eyes expressed a cold sadness.

"Are you happy here?"

"When I was a girl I wanted to convert to Christianity. I went to a Catholic school. The church appealed to me, but my father stopped me. Before he died I promised him never to convert." She spoke as if she was confessing her deepest secrets.

"And you can't break that promise?"

"Not I," said Trude, and her face seemed to tighten. The cold look returned to her eyes.

"I understand," said Lotte.

Trude rose to her feet, wrung out the cloth, and without another word she turned into the lobby and went straight to the kitchen.

The next day Mirzel announced that she was leaving. She was twenty-nine years old. The two years she had spent in the retreat had transformed her utterly. She had grown fat and spoke in a German-Jewish accent. She had learned more than she had taught. She had learned to speak in a whisper, say thank you and I beg your pardon, and to wear city clothes. At the time, she had inherited Sophia's clothes, and more recently Isadora's. She had entered into a number of temporary liaisons with the residents. These affairs had left no traces of resentment in her heart. On the contrary, she remembered them with secret affection. Naturally, she also cheated, told lies and stole a little jewelry, but none of these things helped her to keep her figure. Now she looked like one of the female residents of the retreat, younger, but no less spoiled. In the course of time she had learned to appreciate a slab of chocolate, a glass of liqueur and even to long for the plains.

"Why are you going, aren't you happy here?"

She did not know what to say. She had grown accustomed even to Trude's persecution.

"Are you homesick?"

"No." This was the unvarnished truth. Her father was strict, her mother blind, her elder sisters treated her like a servant.

"In that case, why are you leaving?"

"I don't know." And this too was the truth. Sometimes she would ask herself: What am I doing here with these Jews? I'm a Christian born and bred. What have I to do with them? As a young girl she had gone to church to pray, but ever since her mother went blind she had begun to lie: I've been to church already. Or, I'm going in a little while.

She had grown accustomed to the way of life here, to the eccentricities of the residents and their little self-indulgences. Lauffer, as usual, was severely practical and said, "Think hard. The village isn't paradise either." He had good reasons for saying this. He had spent many a pleasant summer night with Mirzel in the forest. But Mirzel had made up her mind, she was leaving at the end of the month. It was not the fault of the residents, or even of Balaban's illness. But bad dreams attacked her in the night, her blind mother appeared and ordered her to come home. To tell the truth, her mother had been telling her to come home for two months already. And Mirzel would say, in a little while, in a little while. But she did not keep her word.

And thus the coaxing came to an end. Each of them came and offered up his gift. Mrs. Kron brought her a fine piece of jewelry, made by an artist in solid silver. Lauffer went down to the village and bought her a fur coat. Everyone brought something. Some gave cash and some jewelry.

Mirzel stood there embarrassed, blushing at the shower of gifts. Apart from these gifts, her room was crammed with the things she had received, stolen or inherited over the years, but she was obviously moved nevertheless. In the end Rauch delivered a short speech in his own name and on behalf of all the inmates. He said, "We are all grateful for your loyal services, your devoted care. You have helped us a great deal. You have taught us much." He spoke in the manner to which he had been accustomed in the bank, in the words which he had acquired there, but nevertheless they now sounded heartfelt and genuine, perhaps because they were spoken in the hall, and perhaps because of Balaban's groans, which were clearly audible.

Mirzel for her part said, "Thank you. Thank you from the bottom of my heart. I'll never forget you. You will all be engraved upon my heart for ever." And she immediately burst into tears. They all ran up to embrace and console her. And while this wave of emotion flooded the hall, Herbert rose to his feet and announced: "Mirzel will come and visit us. We are not saying goodbye forever. We are people after all, not mountains."

This consolation had its effect: Mirzel quieted down, gathered up her gifts, packed her suitcases, put on Sophia's winter clothes, made up her face and went to stand on the front steps. She looked like an attractive middle-class woman who had ordered a carriage to go to pay a family call. Now too a number of emotional words were spoken, warm and choked. But Mirzel's thoughts were already elsewhere.

Soon afterward Herbert appeared with the cart. Robert helped her to lift her many cases. The following thought crossed his mind: This servant girl is putting on the airs of a great lady. She doesn't even lift a finger to help load her heavy cases onto the cart. And when the cart moved off at last he did not even bother to raise his head.

NINETEEN

Balaban's illness grew worse. Once a week the converted doctor came to examine him and prescribe medicines. He came and went with the regularity of a clock ticking in an endless gray mist. What was there to say? The words rang hollow as a pendulum in a sealed old box.

But for Betty people would have sunk into their own reflections, but she never stopped talking, telling stories and pouring out her intimate confessions, a ceaseless stream of chatter which embraced past and present, her father and her mother, her ex-husband and her girlhood friends. If only she had married an Austrian born and bred her life would have been different, but her father, although he himself was not observant, had forced her to marry a Jew. And the Jews, begging their pardon, understood nothing about music and the theater.

"Nor do the Austrians," said Lauffer carelessly.

"You're making a big mistake," retorted Betty in a voice which was not lacking in importance.

"No, madam, I know them only too well."

"And how do you account for the fact that my parents stopped me from studying acting and forced me to marry a Jew even though I didn't love him?"

"Because you are a Jew yourself. Jewish stupidity must go on."

"I may be a Jew by birth, but not by temperament."

"Austrians, madam, only make their confessions in front of a priest and on their deathbeds."

"Jews have been at the bottom of all my troubles. I never had a chance to study. They never let me study. They corrupted my character."

"Study what?"

"Why the theater, of course, music and the plastic arts."

"You haven't got any talent."

"You should be ashamed of yourself. Of course I've got talent. Everybody says so."

Strange, nobody was angry with Betty any more. These conversations, exposed and empty, filled the air with a dull noise. Lotte sat and listened, as if someone had placed a magnifying mirror before her eyes. She too, to tell the truth, was drawn to them as if by magic—it was never the Jews who appealed to her heart, only the tall, blond Austrians, in each of whom she imagined she could see an artist. True, her mother had not prevented her from going on the stage, but it was only the sick ambition of a Jewish mother to see her daughter famous. Never mind at what.

The thought crossed her mind that people are not as different from one another as we sometimes think.

Lotte felt a faint stirring of sympathy for this fat woman everyone contemptuously called Betty the babbler. For years, ever since she was a girl, she had been trying to escape her fate, a weak woman with unsteady nerves, and now she no longer had the strength even to keep her most intimate secrets to herself. One desire still remained to her: Robert. But this aging peasant had already had his fill of women.

"You don't seem to like the Jews."

"No, I don't," she said. "Certainly not. Let others like them. Not me."

"Why?"

"Because they're weak. Unstable."

"So what?"

"They lack the beauty of nature. They're born in grocery shops. Among the barrels and the sacks."

Thus Lauffer sat and teased her. The people at the tables no longer reacted. Since Balaban's illness had taken a turn for the worse he no longer shouted or cursed. Trude and Herbert took care of him devotedly.

In Lotte's life the clamor quietened. For hours on end she sat in the hall. Herbert's checked suit was faded, there were dark grease stains on his shoes. He spoke little, and when he spoke to Trude in the kitchen he sounded painfully practical. There were no potatoes and no beetroot. Rauch's suit too lost its shape. He sat in the kitchen peeling squash. He did his work to Trude's satisfaction. Lang too had found the right rhythm in his morning runs. He did not stop preaching, but his sermons were no longer angry. Why don't you go out for a morning run? A morning run revives the spirits. That summer he intended buying a cabin in the village. A cow, and a piece of land. The Jews had done a lot of harm, to themselves and others. Commerce had ruined their characters. Only the land could cure them now. And although he sang the same tune every day, nobody told him to keep quiet. Perhaps because his words sounded like some dull, endless drone, incapable of doing any harm to anybody.

TWENTY

Balaban died at the end of March. It was a fine day, with no wind blowing on the still, snowy slopes. There was a transparency in the air. From the wide front window the plain spread out below as far as the eye could see, until it was swallowed up in a sea of mist.

During his last few days he was quiet. He hardly complained at all. From time to time, at night, a word in his mother tongue escaped his lips, but apart from these not a murmur. It was hard to imagine Balaban leaving life. Even in his severe illness he had not seemed like a sick man.

Betty burst into tears. People stood next to her and comforted her as if it were her own personal tragedy. Herbert was quiet and matter of fact and went out to look for a suitable place to bury him. Wrapped in his winter coat he looked like a merchant whose wide-ranging business interests imposed restraint on him even in the hour of his distress. Lang muttered, "He was a great man. We never appreciated his greatness. He was a generation ahead of his time. We have to admit, we never plumbed the depths of his thought."

As always now there was no lack of grief that was skin deep, crocodile tears and lip service. Herbert made the necessary arrangements without ceremony. He went down to the cellar and brought up three spades, an ax and a pick. These crude implements stood in the doorway and showed more than anything that the spirit, or whatever we like to call it, is not divorced from the body.

They dug the grave in the ice-covered ground, and the funeral was consequently postponed until the last light of the setting sun. The digging was hard work, and those who took part in it came back dirty and sweating and immediately began to make practical arrangements: they brought up the stretcher and the blanket, all the things which had been used for previous funerals too. Robert cut wood for the sign.

Now again they saw the clear slopes, the bare trees planted unsteadily in the snow. Lotte kept to the rear, in order to avoid Herbert's eye. She was afraid that she would be called upon again to stand up and read. This little fear accompanied her

146

throughout the procession. The path was slippery and the stretcher-bearers tripped and stumbled a number of times. But Lotte was unaware of these incidents; she was afraid and angry at herself for not being able to overcome this weakness.

Lang wept. In his dirty athletic attire he looked like a poor day laborer with not a penny in his pocket to show for his work. He wept not only for Balaban's death but also for his funeral. He deserved a different funeral, an athletic funeral. And when he said this he looked even more pathetic than before. His short sleeves exposed his skinny arms, blue with cold.

Trude did not take part in the funeral. The moment she heard the news she packed her bags without a word to anyone and left. To her credit, it must be said that in the last days she had not stirred from his bedside, like a devoted sister. Everyone knew that she was busy tending him day and night. And let it be said to her credit too—before she left she cleaned the shelves, polished the pots and wrote a few practical instructions down on the notice board.

And as at every funeral, what was there to say? How was it possible to keep silent? No one came to Herbert's aid. Herbert bowed his head and eulogized Balaban. He spoke of Balaban's great dreams in simple, practical terms. It was plain that his many trips to the village, the buying and the selling, had taught him words he had never used before. Life was nothing grand or glorious, but since we had been given it we were not at liberty to despise it. Balaban had tried to teach them this wisdom. It was not easy to learn from him, but his intentions had been serious. He had lost all his property.

As at previous funerals, Robert wore a black band on his sleeve but he now looked no different from the others. He wore a suit which one of the residents had given him when he left. In this suit he looked like a retired clerk who kept the whole of his small income in his waistcoat pocket, out of suspicion and fear. Even his hands had grown pale, as if they had never seen the sun.

The people climbed the smooth slope, slipping and holding onto each other. The sun lingered above the horizon and the sky was clear and pure. And as always, this time too a number of remarks were made which were ugly in their nakedness. Like Hammer, for instance, who did not restrain himself and said, "It was no dream, but a delusion. Let a man do what he has to do without making a fuss. And first of all, let him look out for himself. We were not intended for great things. My experience has taught me that a man who takes care of himself first may have something left over for others. Let nobody expect any favors." His tone was as smug as that of a petit-bourgeois businessman talking to his sons and daughters who wanted to save the world. And that was exactly what he looked like too. Short, slightly round-shouldered, and horribly gray.

Afterward they stood at the doorway as if they were afraid of going inside. The light poured down cold and blue as if it were the beginning of winter. Herbert wasted no time. He went straight into the stable, fed the horse and gave it water, cleaned the floor and laid down a bed of straw. He wanted to groom the horse too, but night suddenly fell and there was utter darkness in the stable.

And as after every funeral—thirst. They were all thirsting for a cup of hot coffee. Strange, Betty of all people, who had not stopped wailing and screaming all morning long, was now the first to say, I'll make the coffee. Sit down everybody and leave it to me.

The sight of the clean kitchen, the utensils hanging on their hooks and the explicit instructions which Trude had left behind her, brought a practical gleam back to Betty's grieving eyes: to prepare and serve a meal. And she did it efficiently too, like a practiced housewife. In no time at all the steaming pots of coffee and plates of hot sandwiches arrived on the tables. The cold hall was suddenly filled with homely vapors. Betty's hands were full of work. It was evident that the work made her happy. The grief of the others also was eased by the hot food.

Only Lang refused to be consoled. His thin, unshaven face showed more clearly than words that

149

his world had collapsed. Lotte, for some reason, sat at the table and wrote a letter to her daughter. She told her at length about the grant she had been awarded, so that she was no longer in need of any assistance. Her needs were now taken care of. She wrote quietly, above all in order to ease her daughter's conscience. Lately she had sensed that Julia was about to come and visit her and she truly wanted to see her face, but not to cause her unnecessary sorrow.

And thus life resumed its normal course. The inmates, for the time being, found relief in talking. They talked of the past and the present, about the affairs of the retreat, and even about politics. And for a moment the place seemed like a poor roadside inn where people find a temporary shelter for the night.

Now Hammer was as practical as ever. He ate one sandwich and wrapped the other in wax paper to take up to his room. People should eat no more than was necessary. Who knew what tomorrow would bring? Lotte sat and watched them closely: of all her many friends and relatives only these were left to her. Not particularly close, but people who could be relied on in time of trouble. This realization wrapped her for a moment in a veil of sadness.

That night they went to bed early. In the hall an oil lamp flickered and diffused a dim light. Lang sat in the armchair, wearing the striped gym pants he had worn to the funeral. When he saw Lotte he rose to his feet.

150

"You're sitting by yourself," said Lotte in surprise.

"I can't pull myself together."

"It was a blow to us all," said Lotte, in the way people say.

Lang bowed his head. The expression on his thin, tormented face was one of boyish earnestness.

Lotte said, "He was different from the rest of us."

"He was a completely simple man. The final simplicity, I should say. He understood that without a drastic change we have no hope, we're lost. And it all fell to pieces because the disciples rose against their mentor. Believe me, madam, much will still be said about his simplicity. How he tried to build a wall against the coming flood. His vision was appallingly simple. Isn't simplicity one of the signs of greatness?"

Lotte sensed that the man was speaking out of his own deepest pain.

"Pardon me, madam," he said. "Pardon me for talking too much. By doing so I have offended not only you, but also the memory of Balaban." As he said this he seemed to stand exposed in all his shame: a man who talked too much. Without another word he turned away and went into his room.

Lotte sat in the empty hall. She too was tired and dazed but she was not sleepy. The scenes of the day mingled with the scenes of her past, but the past came to her more clearly.

When did it begin? she asked herself absentmind-

151

edly. When I left home? I had no love for my parents' home. When that scoundrel seduced me? But I was attracted to him. When I married? I didn't want to get married. She asked the qustions and answered them as if she were on the witness stand.

Afterward, in bed, the questions and answers did not stop, but gradually they turned into pictures. Each picture with its own colors. Until the colors of the night encompassed her and she sunk into them as if she were diving into deep water.

TWENTY-ONE

And as the snow thawed, gray and grubby and in-
glorious, as if she were rising out of a thick mist—
Julia appeared. She stood in the doorway, heavy
and bundled in a peasant's coat. Lotte hardly recognized her. But it was Julia. The past year had
changed her beyond recognition. Her narrow,
strained face had grown fleshy and her mouth was
open in an awkward smile. To tell the truth, ever
since Lotte had written her letter she had stopped
thinking about Julia. Every now and then her
daughter would appear to her, but these appearances held no sadness. Lotte was preoccupied with
herself and the day-to-day life of the retreat.

A few days before she had once again received
regards from her ex-husband, Manfred. He also had

undergone vicissitudes. He was now living in another little town, and there too he was playing in a Jewish band. What does it mean, a Jewish band, she asked herself in passing, but she did not pause to ponder this question.

"What brought you here?" asked Lotte, overcome by embarrassment.

"Nothing," Julia blurted out. She bent down and removed the following things from her bag: a few jars of jam, a bottle of oil, two loaves of bread and dried fruit wrapped in a white cloth.

"I'm so glad," said Lotte. "But why so much?"

At the sound of these words Julia took the heavy peasant shawl off her head and her face was revealed in all its fullness. There were a few red marks on her neck. Her hands too were broad and fleshy.

"Why did you go to so much trouble?"

"It's nothing," she said in a heavy country voice.

"I'm quite all right," said Lotte.

Julia's face grew more and more exposed.

"And what is George doing, and the children?"

"Working."

"I'm very glad."

It occurred to Lotte that something had happened inside Julia. She had never reacted in this way before. Her whole being breathed heaviness.

"And what have you been doing with yourself?"

"Working."

Herbert appeared in the hall and Lotte called out

154

to him: "Herbert, I have a visitor. Julia has come to visit me." And Herbert, who was in a good humor, said, "Your mother is doing very well here. You will still hear great things of her." At the sound of these words Julia bared her teeth, broad, healthy teeth.

It was afternoon. The spring sun pierced the windows and dappled the floor with light. The hall was now exposed in all its poverty. A few people were sitting at the tables playing cards. Mrs. Kron was sitting in the armchair where Isadora used to sit.

"So we haven't been completely forgotten," said Herbert jokingly.

Julia did not respond. The heavy peasant coat thickened her figure and made her seem impermeable.

"And how did you get here?" said Lotte wonderingly.

"I have a cart."

At the sound of these words Lotte hurried to the window. And indeed, there stood a horse and cart, of the kind used for transporting hay.

"Wonderful," said Lotte, as if a miracle had occurred.

For two months they had not seen a stranger on the mountain. People had stopped writing letters and no letters came for them. The long, cold winter had accustomed them to their isolation.

"And George is working on the farm."

"He's working hard," said Julia weightily.

"And is he still drinking?"

"Oh yes, he's still drinking." Julia smiled.

"But not beating you, I hope."

Julia bared her teeth again and her smile became even more awkward than before.

Their conversation, for some reason, was conducted loudly, in the doorway to the hall, and attracted the attention of the people inside. And although they did not look as if they were eavesdropping they were indeed eavesdropping.

"I'll bring you a cup of coffee," said Lotte, and hurried into the kitchen.

Julia sat down and drank in silence. And Lotte, who did not wish there to be a silence between them, told her at length and in a loud voice about the grant she had been awarded by the board, a grant which enabled her to devote herself entirely to her art. The flood of words seemed beyond Julia's grasp. She sat and listened, but without concentrating.

"And is everything all right at home?" Lotte tried once more to make her daughter talk.

"Everything's all right," said Julia in a matter-of-fact tone, as if she were exchanging a word with a neighbor in the grocery shop.

It was Julia but at the same time it was not her. As if her being had been encased in heavy armor. Lotte had met such women on her travels, standing at the doors of their houses or on the riverbanks. Dull, submissive as domestic animals. Incapable of uttering a word.

156

For a long time she sat without asking questions and without looking at her. And the longer she sat there the more she felt the pressure of the words collecting in her throat, wanting to burst out. And like her mother before her, she too said, "You should take a long holiday, have a little rest. You're very tired."

Julia's face exchanged one set of lines for another, but it remained heavy and expressionless. Now some peasant cunning, learned in the fields, seemed to rise and flood her lips, and she said, "Never mind." A world of rustic wisdom and equanimity was contained in these two words.

"Pardon me," said Lotte.

Julia rose to her feet and said, "I must go now, Mother." She pronounced the word "mother" like a peasant woman visiting her aged mother.

"And what are the children doing?" Lotte tried to hang onto her.

"They're all right. They're working in the fields with George."

"Won't you come and see me again?"

"I'll come in the summer, after the harvest."

Lotte suddenly saw a picture of peasants scattered in a field, singing and shouting at the top of their voices. It occurred to her that in the evening when George came home tired and drunk he brought his whip down on Julia, as he brought it down on his farm animals.

"George beats you, doesn't he?"

"What of it," said Julia in a cold, quiet voice, as if

157

someone had touched an old wound which had already healed.

"What are you saying? I won't allow it."

"Mother." Julia took Lotte's arm. "All women are beaten. They don't die of it."

"No," said Lotte, covering her mouth anxiously with her hand.

"It's nothing," said Julia, as if they were speaking of a couple of chickens caught by a fox, and there was no point in crying over spilled milk. Lotte took both her hands in hers.

"Will you come again in the summer?"

"At the end of summer."

Julia bent down and kissed her on the forehead, as people kissed in the country. Without undue passion or excitement.

"I'll leave you now," she said. Lotte accompanied her to the cart.

"It's not bad here. What do the people do?" she surprised Lotte by asking.

"Nothing in particular."

"They don't work?"

"No."

"What do they do, then?"

"Nothing."

"Strange," said Julia, and she smiled. And with no more questions she broadened her step, climbed onto the seat and cracked her whip. The cart moved off and rumbled down the hill.

Lotte remained standing where she was. The

slopes shone, white and polished. All the cold of the winter was absorbed in them. She stood there without moving for a long time. For some reason, she now remembered the first summer she had spent with Manfred. Even then it had been clear to her that her marriage with Manfred would not last long, and nevertheless it had lasted for years. Now Manfred was living in a remote little town and playing in a Jewish band.

TWENTY-TWO

After this a sense of well-being descended on the retreat, a time of grace. Betty worked in the kitchen and served hot meals without adhering to a strict timetable. The meals were meager but tasty. At long last Betty had come into her own. The desire to feed people with hot meals gave her face a grave, womanly importance. She worked hard but her work brought many compensations. Everyone praised her cooking.

The burden fell on Herbert's thin shoulders. He was always coming and going, going down to the village and bringing up provisions. He did not bring much. And what he brought Betty would divide up and ration out in installments. Herbert's face gradually took on the expression of a workingman. His intellectual horizons shrank to the simplest acts.

160

The retreat now resembled a poor but clean hotel. Betty worked till late at night but there was always a pot of tea on the counter. People drank whenever they felt like it.

And thus the spring passed. It was cold but no one complained or moralized. As if they had all agreed that change was impossible and their fate in any case was sealed. Superfluous words would get them nowhere.

But even in these last days passions did not die down completely. From time to time someone would remember and ask in surprise: What am I doing here? All my property is down below. My daughter is down below. What am I waiting for?

"Is it so bad here?"

"No, to tell the truth. But I feel uneasy."

Even Engel, even that self-torturer, who never stopped practicing all winter, suddenly said one evening, "My playing has improved. I'm ready to go back to the orchestra. They'll be glad to see the improvement."

Betty too, full of her new activities, did not hide her envy of Lotte. "You're an actress, you've worked in the theater. And me, what am I? I grew up in a poor Jewish home. I was married young to a man without character. Nothing came of all my dreams. I love the peasants. They're strong and healthy. But what can I do, they never loved me."

But the complaints were not serious. People went quietly about their business. Those who did not work in the kitchen worked in the yard. Trees grew

161

in the yard and spread a pleasant shade. Lang cleaned the gym and fixed it up. The inmates did not exercise, but Lang thought that for Balaban's sake the gym should be put in order. The light in the front yard was soft and it was gradually enclosed in a cover of green leaves.

Lotte now remembered her arrival on the mountain clearly, the coach and the coachman, Julia sitting in the corner, tight-lipped, her brow dark and her hands red and swollen with water. It all looked cold and remote to her now, although the proportions seemed right and the colors not exaggerated. And she remembered Lang too, in his short gym pants, standing at the front entrance, thin and joyless, a corporal in an anonymous army of reserves. She saw Herbert too. His checked suit, elegantly negligent, inspiring confidence.

Now Herbert got up early in the morning, harnessed the horse to the cart and went down to the village. Anyone who had a jacket or a pair of trousers or a shirt worth selling gave it to him to sell. There was no need to ask. People gave generously and in a kind of secret desire to get rid of superfluous baggage. The days were fine and clear, and from day to day they grew clearer.

From time to time Herbert was joined by Rauch or Hammer. And when they came back at night they looked neither cheerful nor somber. Their movements were measured and uniform. The provisions were scant but neatly packed, and Betty greeted them with a maternal air.

Outside it was warm and pleasant. It was possible to sit on the slopes and look around and reflect: Not far from here busy cities exist, trams drive back and forth, people get up early to go to work, a clerk opens his counter, a maid takes off her shoes so as not to enter the house with mud from the countryside. One detail after the other, as if filtered through a fine sieve. One thing was clear: these things no longer belonged to us.

Lotte's sorrow grew duller. True, she never stopped thinking, seeing and remembering, but her thoughts were without anger. She worked five or six hours in the kitchen and then she sat on the slopes. And as always, she never stopped thinking about her body, her wrinkles and blemishes. Her jars of cosmetics were empty and this grieved her. Now too it was important to her to look her best.

It was true that people had not changed, but Balaban's death had brought them closer to each other. Not an absolute closeness. From time to time they would recall him as a riddle which refused to be solved. Lang stopped talking about him in bombastic words. From time to time a quarrel broke out over trifles. For the most part the quarrels died down of their own accord.

And the summer grew broad and hot. Herbert now returned from the village beaten and wounded. Ruffians fell on him and beat him up. His appearance toward evening was excruciating in its silence. Betty tended his wounds with wet compresses.

The pain was cruel, the shame terrible, but Herbert got up every morning and went out to endure his suffering. The provisions he brought back were scant, but nevertheless their meager meals were eaten in tranquillity. Later, they began to take turns, and Rauch and Lauffer would go down in his place. They too were beaten and their wounds were bandaged by Betty.

The world seemed to be narrowing down to its simplest dimensions: breakfast, supper. And if anyone said, I would like—all he had in mind was a cup of coffee. Sins were not pardoned, sentences were not commuted, but no one threw them in the face of his fellows. Their only worry now was that the cart might fail to return from the village.

And when all the coats had been sold, the jewels and the suits, Herbert went into Balaban's room, sorted out his clothes and tied them up in a sheet. Tomorrow he would sell them to the farmers. At night, of course, people were afraid. But they helped one another. If a man fell or was beaten he was not abandoned.

ABOUT THE AUTHOR

Aharon Appelfeld was eight when he witnessed the murder of his mother by the Nazis. After escaping from a concentration camp, he wandered in the forests for two years. When the war ended he joined the Soviet Army as a kitchen boy, eventually emigrating to Palestine in 1946. The author of eleven internationally acclaimed novels, including *Badenheim 1939*, *The Age of Wonders*, *Tzili*, *To the Land of the Cattails*, and *Katerina*, he lives in Jerusalem.

GREAT LITERATURE FROM
SCHOCKEN BOOKS

A Book That Was Lost and Other Stories by S. Y. Agnon
Edited by Alan Mintz and Anne Golomb Hoffman
0-8052-1066-0

Tevye the Dairyman and the Railroad Stories
Sholem Aleichem
Translated and with an introduction by Hillel Halkin
0-8052-1069-5

The Iron Tracks by Aharon Appelfeld
0-8052-4158-2

Unto the Soul by Aharon Appelfeld
0-8052-1097-0

The Castle by Franz Kafka
A new translation, based on the restored text
0-8052-4118-3

The Periodic Table by Primo Levi
0-8052-1041-5

The Schocken Book of Contemporary Jewish Fiction
Edited by Ted Solotaroff and Nessa Rapoport
0-8052-1065-2

The Gates of the Forest by Elie Wiesel
0-8052-1044-X

AVAILABLE AT YOUR LOCAL BOOKSTORE, OR CALL TOLL-FREE:
1-800-733-3000 (CREDIT CARDS ONLY).

CENTRAL

AUG 0 5 2005

DEC 27 2005

OCT 09 2010

GAYLORD

PRINTED IN U.S.A.